Dark Anonymous Confessions

Vincent V. Cava

Edited by
Kirsten Milliron

The Author

Vincent V. Cava

His tales have been known to induce seizures in small children. Merely skimming through one of his stories can lead to anxiety, nausea, and internal bleeding. You should not read anything written by him if you are currently pregnant or nursing (including this author's bio...although it's probably too late by now). He's a man whose mind is so dark, not even the World-Wide-Web could contain his horrific imagination.

He is Vincent V. Cava!

The son of NASA researchers, Vincent V. Cava's writing has quickly amassed a following over the Internet. His stories have been translated into dozens of different languages and have been used to promote major studio films. You can find out more about Vincent by following him on Facebook, Instagram, or Twitter.

You may also subscribe to his mailing list for FREE exclusive stories and promos.

Table of Contents

The Pastel Man

To My Dear Son, Mathew,

I can't imagine how strange it must feel to receive a letter written a decade ago from your father who has long since been dead. Don't be cross with your Aunt for withholding it from you all these years. She was simply honoring my wishes. She's a good woman and I'm sure that she and your Uncle Benjamin have done a wonderful job raising you in the absence of your mother and I.

I merely wanted to wait until you were old enough to fully grasp what I am about to tell you. I also did not want to burden you while you were still a boy with the information that I will be imparting to you – on this your eighteenth birthday. A child should not be forced to bare the weight of their father's past mistakes.

It's funny, eighteen is such an arbitrary number, but this day does carry some significance. It represents your transition from a boy into a man. From today on forward you are expected to have your own responsibilities, create your own experiences, and endure your own hardships. Your Aunt and Uncle will always be there for you, but if they raised you to be as strong as I expect them to, then you should be able to handle yourself out in the real world just fine. It is that reason that I chose this day to reveal to you the circumstances surrounding my death.

That being said, disclosing to you the cause and reason of my passing only helps to satisfy half the aim of this letter. The other is to serve as a caveat, in hopes that I can prevent you from making the same mistake that I did that cold winter night, kneeling beside my father's writhing body on the living room floor. So I prey that you heed my warning, son, and read this cautionary tale with an open mind. If for whatever reason you forget everything else I've ever told you, then I beg that you remember this one thing. In the event that it ever comes to you during a moment of weakness, as it did me all those years ago, say no to the Pastel Man. It doesn't matter how much you love the person that it promises to help, nothing is worth what it wants in return.

It was 1985 when I first encountered the creature, well before you were born, but ever since, not a day has gone by where its awful face hasn't haunted my thoughts. I was a teenager then, but I look at that evening as the night my childhood died – corrupted and violated by a callous hell beast with pale blue skin.

Even though it happened years ago, I still remember the events of that fateful first encounter vividly. I could tell you what my father and I were wearing, the toppings on the pizza we were eating, even the score of the football game playing on the TV. It was around half time when my father's speech started to become slurred, which I found odd since he had been nursing the same bottle of beer since kickoff.

Stranger even, I had seen him drink a six-pack to himself in the past without even appearing tipsy so I was having trouble understanding how a single drink could have such an effect on him. I realized it wasn't the alcohol when half his body went limp and he slid off the couch. I asked him if he was all right, but his words had now become incomprehensible so I grabbed the phone off the coffee table and dialed 911.

"911, what's your emergency?"

"I think my Dad's having a stroke." The thought had only crossed my mind a second before the operator answered the phone.

"Ok, we have your address. An ambulance is on its way. It should be there soon. Is he conscious?" The operator's voice was calm, yet frustratingly distant – almost apathetic in a way. Here I was, a teenage boy traumatized and terrified, and the person on the other line was speaking to me as if it was just another day at the office.

Where's the empathy? I remember thinking. *Where's the concern? A man is dying!*

"Yes. He's conscious, but I can't understand him." I responded.

Nonsensical jumbled sounds were spilling out my father's mouth. I was afraid. He was all I had. My mother passed away when I was a baby so I never got the chance to know her, but my dad was always there – doing the job of two parents. If I lost him, then I knew I'd be alone.

"That's normal with strokes. It's good that he's awake – " And I didn't hear the rest because that's when I dropped the phone.

I was having one of those moments where everything faded into the background while my world fell silent. The football game playing on the television, the operator giving me instructions over the phone, even the sound of my father's voice as he wailed in agony on the carpet became white noise – dissolving into the air as I lost all awareness of my surroundings. All of my attention and focus was now on one thing. The horrible abomination that was standing in my kitchen, watching my father and I with a twisted smile across its disgusting face.

Its head narrowly missed scraping against our kitchen's 9ft ceiling as it shifted from side to side, fidgeting with anticipation like a giddy child in class on the last day of school waiting for that final bell to signal summer vacation. The pastel blue skin that covered its entire body, from the creature's head all the way down to its feet horrible grimy feet, looked weathered and wrinkled like leather that had been left out in the sun for days. Hanging off its long, lanky frame was a plain brown satchel with black stitching. It lightly caressed the strap of its pouch with a long finger while it looked on with an eager expression on its face.

I had also quickly become aware of a drastic increase in temperature. Beads of sweat began collecting on my forehead. The room was now as warm as a sauna. The air too had changed. It was thicker, heavier, and much harder to breath. It felt as though the living room had suddenly adopted the climate of the Amazon Rain Forest.

At first I thought I had gone mad from the sight of seeing my father have a stroke, but the closer the monstrosity slinked towards us, the more I realized it was no hallucination. It ducked its head under the light fixture in the living room and stepped a spindly leg over the couch. Though the monstrous freak of nature was clearly bipedal, it had moved down to all fours and appeared to be stalking us like some kind of wild animal hunting its prey. I should have been terrified, but the god-awful smile on its face made me feel more anger towards the thing than fear. It was as if it was taking pleasure in my father's misery. Closer still it crept and I grabbed my father's hand out of desperation in some veiled attempt to protect him. The creature stopped its face mere inches from mine before shifting its attention down to my father and uttering a string of words that have forever changed my life.

"I can save him, if you'd like?"

I was taken aback. I had prepared for the terrible thing to bite a chunk of flesh out of my neck or dig its black crust covered nails into my face, but speaking to me was the last thing I expected.

"He's dying, but I can save him. If you'd like?"

I sat there, mouth agape, cradling my father's head in my arm and staring into the two pink bulbous eyes that took up more than a third of the foul thing's face. I remember thinking that they reminded me of Easter Eggs – a bizarre connection for my mind to make given the situation. It stood back up on two feet and once again I was reminded just how physically imposing the creature really was. It told me its name, which I dare not repeat because it also explained that speaking it would summon the beast. For the remainder of my story I will refer to this entity as the Pastel Man – just a name I came up with due to the pigment of its skin and the light shade of pink that was the color of its eyes. That and for some reason using such a foolish title to refer to the creature always helped to make me feel less afraid of it. Not much though. *Not much at all.*

Finally, my mind had recovered enough from shock to allow me to stutter out a few words, "What do you mean you can save him?"

"What I do is make deals, young man." Its voice was surprisingly angelic – like a thousand choirs all singing in unison. If one were to close their eyes while the creature spoke to them, they might imagine they were listening to a seraph, not the hideous monster sporting a depraved grin in my living room. However, its extraordinary voice only managed to make me more uneasy. It wasn't right that something so beautiful would belong to such a repulsive creature.

The Pastel Man gestured to its satchel. "I have the ability to save your father's life, but we'll need to come to an arrangement first."

"What kind of a arrangement?"

"Everything happens for a reason, even death." Its mischievous smile widened just a bit as if the creature was getting to the punch line of a joke. "It's true that I can save your father's life, but someone must die in his place. One *must* die, so another can live. That's the deal." I clutched my chest. "Not you, what would be the point? No, no, no, I'm giving you the option to choose the person who will be replacing your father this evening."

I was stunned by what I was hearing. Feeling woozy from the heat, I wiped some sweat from my brow in an attempt to stall long enough to recollect myself.

"Are you death?" I asked.

The Pastel Man threw its head back and let out terrible howl. It was only later that I would come to realize that was how the wretched thing laughed. "No, I'm certainly not The Grim Reaper, although you aren't the first person to ask me that. I'm not the devil either, nor do I work for him. Let's just say I'm an independent contractor, shall we?" Two tiny holes that lied on the center of its face in the absence of a nose flared in satisfaction of its explanation.

"I can choose anyone?"

"Well, not anyone. That wouldn't be very fun, would it?" I could see a row of shark like teeth hiding in its mouth as it separated its lips to speak. "Your father's replacement must be someone else in your life."

"I'm not a murderer." My voice was tiny and barely escaped my mouth. I looked back down to my father. He had lost consciousness and his skin was becoming pale. "And I don't think I could kill anyone I know."

"You won't have to get your hands dirty, young man." The sly creature was moving into its final pitch. "All you have to do is tell me who it is you want dead and I will do the rest. Surely there must be someone you wouldn't mind out of your life? A teacher, an ex-girlfriend, a nasty neighbor perhaps?"

There was one. I had fantasized about it many times, but never in my wildest dreams would I have ever acted on it. Everyone has that toxic person in their life. Someone who makes getting up in the morning more difficult and I was certainly no exception. "Walter Flannigan," I muttered under my breath.

"Who?"

"Walter Flannigan. He's the guy at school who gave me this." I lifted my shirt and showed it the handprint shaped bruise on my chest that Walter had given me during one of his infamous "hazing sessions" in the locker room earlier that week. "He's been shoving me into lockers, and beating me up since I was a freshman. The faculty doesn't do anything about it since he's the biggest football recruit to ever come out of my school. He's already committed to play for a major university next year. Sports Illustrated even did a piece on him."

"Ahhh," The Pastel Man began to snicker to itself. It somehow widened its already enormous pink eyes even more then crouched back down to get face to face with me again. "What fun is being a king, without peasants to torment, eh?"

"Well I'm tired of being tormented so just go and kill him before I change my mind!"

The Pastel Man shot a massive hand out and wrapped its long fingers around my face. The grin that it wore since I had first laid eyes on it had now replaced by a scowl.

"YOU DO NOT TELL ME WHAT TO DO! ARE WE CLEAR?!" I nodded sheepishly.

The grip it had on my face was so tight. I understood then and there that if it wanted to, the creature could easily snap my neck or crush my skull like an egg. My heart began to pound so loud that you could have heard it from the street.

"Good," it continued. "Because it's not so simple, young man. There are steps that must be taken."

"Steps?"

"Yes," A playful smirk once again returned to the Pastel Man's face. "You will have to be present when this Walter Flannigan dies. In fact, I need you to summon me or else I can't complete my end of the bargain. Get the boy alone, there must be no other witnesses, then speak my name. You must watch him die by sunrise or else you will be violating the terms of our agreement. So do we have a deal?" I nodded again and the monster released its hold of my face before snatching my hand. Its giant paws swallowed my palm as we shook to cement our arrangement. "Excellent! With this handshake our deal is binding, young man."

I watched curiously as the Pastel Man reached into its satchel and fumbled around until it found what it was looking for. In between its repugnant fingers it held a strange looking insect about the size of a quarter. It resembled a beetle, but not the likes of one that I've ever seen. I have never had an affinity for insects. In fact, you could even go so far as to call it a minor phobia of mine, but this beetle was beautiful. Every color of the visible light spectrum was represented on its outer shell. Vibrant yellows, pinks, and greens swirled around in patterns on the insect's back while hypnotic purples, reds, and blues stole my gaze and captured my attention. It was reminiscent of something that one might read about in a fairy tale. The bug buzzed its wings in attempt to flutter away, but could not escape the Pastel Man's grasp. With the creature's free hand, it pushed down on my father's jaw in order to open his mouth.

"What are you doing?" I asked, but the Pastel Man ignored my query. To my horror, it violently stuffed the insect into my father's mouth jamming it down his esophagus with its filthy, dirty, fingers.

The Pastel Man rose once more to its feet. "There, the deed is done. Your father will recover in full. Now it's your turn. Remember, the boy dies by sunrise or the deal is off."

It turned its back to me and began to slither away.

"What if I change my mind?" I asked.

The creature stopped almost mid stride and twisted back around. Again its smile had been supplanted by an angry sneer and I felt even less safe then when it was holding my face in a vice grip earlier.

"Your father's health has already been restored so someone must replace him. *One must die* so another can live. That was the deal. If you fail to complete your end of the bargain then that someone will be you. Believe me when I say this, young man, I don't need to be summoned once our deal has been broken. I will come for you. That is a promise. And when I do, you're going to wish you never crossed me."

With that it continued out the kitchen and through the backdoor. I chased after it, but by the time I got outside into the back yard, the thing had disappeared. The chilly winter air felt like a gift from heaven after being in the sweat box that was my living room, but I didn't have time to enjoy it because it was only a moment later when I spotted the lights of an ambulance as it pulled up across the street from my house. I flagged down the EMTs and led them inside to my father.

***

This is without a doubt the most difficult part of the story to write. How does a man go about confessing his biggest regret in life to his one and only son? It pains me that a terrible decision I made before you were born may dismantle any favorable notions of me that you may have had, but this is one part of my legacy that I cannot hide from you. If I am to protect you, then these words must be said.

It wasn't difficult to find Walter. I knew exactly where he was going to be. For a week a boy from my school named Eddie Gillen had been spreading word about a party he was throwing to celebrate the end of our high school's football season. These sorts of festivities were usually attended by kids who ran in the "popular" circles at my school. Social outcasts like myself weren't welcome and would often be turned away if we tried to show up. I was never much into drinking or mingling with boorish oafs anyways so I didn't mind being excluded from these get-togethers. I was however, certain that it was here that I would find Walter.

I had lost track of time at the hospital while waiting to hear from my father's doctors at the ICU and needed to hurry in order to complete my end of the bargain before the sun came up. It was somewhere around 3:30 AM when I pulled my car up to Eddie Gillen's house. The celebration had somewhat died down and I feared that I had missed my opportunity to catch Walter. My concerns were alleviated when I saw that his raised pick-up truck was still in the driveway. I parked a little ways down the street so my car wouldn't be spotted. Another thought crossed my mind. What if Walter had gotten too drunk and passed out? I tried to think of away to get into Eddie's and get the football star alone long enough for the Pastel Man to do whatever it was the creature had planned. Luckily for me, it wasn't too long before the sports hero stumbled out of Eddie's front door and climbed into his truck. I let out a sigh, having just evaded a potentially challenging hurdle and shifted my car into drive.

He pulled into the street and I followed behind, staying far enough away so that I wouldn't tip him off. He was drunk. Even from the distance I was tailing him, I could see his truck swerving in and out of its lane. The Pastel man's remarkably radiant voice played itself over and over like a heavenly broken record in my mind.

You must watch him die by sunrise

I could feel adrenaline begin to rush through my veins. I was excited – something that both surprised and frightened me. Thoughts of my father had retreated back into the inner recesses of my sub con sciousness. He was a distant memory – my focus was now on Walter and all the torment I had received at his hands. No longer would I be forced to put up with his physical and mental abuse. The power was mine now. With one little word I could end it all. I was Gabriel, my voice was my horn and I needed only sound it to bring Walter's world crumbling down.

My thoughts turned towards the Pastel Man. Oh, how his terrible smile unnerved me. It would most likely be the last thing Walter ever saw. Yet somehow this thought brought me comfort. I was possessed, but not by the Pastel Man or any other ghoulish apparition. It was the spirit of vengeance that had coiled itself around my soul, crushing and squeezing away any lingering trace of innocence left within it.

I looked out my driver side window. A pink ribbon lined the horizon – the very first signs of sunlight making its presence known in the dark evening sky. In a couple hours morning would arrive and I would be too late to summon the demon. Nevertheless, I would see the Pastel Man again, one way or another.

Walter lived up in the foothills outside of town where some of the wealthier people owned homes. He and a friend of mine were neighbors. From time to time I would go up to his house and see Walter in the drive way tossing the pigskin around with his old man. I wondered briefly how his father would react to Walter's death.

Mr. Flannigan was a good man – I knew him well. When my mother passed, there was a dispute with my father and the life insurance agency over her policy. The money he was supposed to receive when she died was held in abeyance. Both of my parents worked and depended on each other's salaries in order to cover the bills. Without that extra income coming in my father quickly found himself swimming in debt. Mr. Flannigan worked at the bank and called in a few favors to get a very fair loan approved for my father even though there was a chance he wouldn't be able to collect on my mother's life insurance. Without that money, my Dad would have been behind on the mortgage and may have lost the house. Once the insurance company finally caved two years later, my father was able to settle his debt with the bank. It was risk that Mr. Flannigan didn't need to take, but did anyways out of the kindness of his heart. Years later he and my father remained friendly and still made small tall when they saw each other around town.

When I asked him once why he put his neck out on the line to approve such a dangerous loan for us, he told me this, "Your father had just lost his wife and you were just a baby. You and Walter are the same age so it wasn't hard to put myself in your old man's his shoes. Sometimes we're so wrapped up in our own problems that we forget to think about others."

I had been consumed with vengeance, but now a sense of guilt was beginning to build inside me for what my actions were about to put Mr. Flannigan through. Those feelings were only fleeting though. Walter was going to pay. I pushed any and all distractions behind me in order to focus on the task at hand.

We had come to a more secluded part of the road that cut through a wooded area so I decided that was where I would make my move. I sped up until I was tailgating the truck then started flashing my brights and honking my horn. I was prepared to rear end the truck in order to get him to pull over, but that wasn't even necessary to get the job done. He must have been panicking because Walter's truck started to swerve violently across the street before running off road and sideswiping a tree.

I rolled up behind his now stalled vehicle and paused for a second before getting out of the car – a moment of hesitation brought on by that tiny bit of innocence the spirit of vengeance had yet to crush. I pictured Mr. Flannigan standing next to Walter's grave, bouquet of carnations and lilies in hand, mourning his only son, but the vengeful spirit within me tightened its grip and my reservations were quickly washed away.

A cold winter breeze whipped across my face. The cool air stung as it nipped at my ears so I zipped up my coat and pulled my hood over my head. I left my headlights on and stood in front of my car so Walter could see me.

"Hey Walter," I shouted out.

It wasn't long before his door jerked open and the inebriated football prodigy dropped out of the cab to the ground below. I could see the gears turning in his intoxicated brain while he slowly pieced together what had just happened. By the time he recognized me the look of confusion on his face had shifted into a picture of rage. Walter stormed across the road towards my car with both fists clenched. Memories of the beatings that I suffered through and the teasing that I had faced darted through my mind. Then those words, spoken by that beautiful, terrifying, otherworldly voice replayed themselves again in my head.

One must die so another can live

They were words that had lost all meaning to me. I could barely remember my father, much less the reason why I had originally agreed to offer up Walter to the creature. I was consumed by hate and I finally had the opportunity to return back all the abuse I had received over the years ten fold. Walter was close now and it was now or never. In an eruption of malice and fury I shouted out the Pastel Man's name directly into Walter's face.

He stopped in his tracks, almost as if he was being physically restrained by my outburst, but quickly gathered himself and shoved me hard against the hood of my car. The Pastel Man was nowhere to be seen. For the second time that evening I wondered if

I had gone insane. The boy grabbed me by my jacket's collar, spun me around and raised his fist. I shut my eyes to brace for impact, but the only thing that struck my face was a powerful wave of heat.

The temperature outside had rapidly increased and I could feel myself begin to sweat profusely inside my coat. I opened my eyes to see Walter's mouth hanging open just as mine had when I first caught sight of the Pastel Man earlier that night. I turned my head just in time to see that unmistakable, long, lanky body slink out of the shadows. It was really going to happen. The Pastel Man was going to kill Walter and it was because of me. I thought that the monster's presence would be a relief, but strangely now all I wanted was for it to go away. All the hate, anger, and rage I had been feeling just moments before had flushed itself from my body entirely. Old man vengeance had packed up, gone home, and left behind the hollowed out husk of a scared little boy with nothing but a broken soul.

I may have been more frightened than Walter. I hadn't anticipated the instant feeling of regret I experienced upon seeing the demon's face. That's when a realization caused my stomach to drop. Walter was about to die *and it was my fault*. And for what? Because he pushed me around in school? I wanted to tell him to run and hide – anything that would give me a chance to right what I had done. I thought that maybe I could talk to the creature, offer myself in his place even, but the only thing I could do was mumble a worthless apology under my breath.

"I'm sorry." I was, but sorry doesn't save lives.

The creature moved in front of my car's headlamps and we could see it more clearly now.

I couldn't take my eyes off of the Pastel Man, but I think that had more to do with not being able to look Walter in the face than fear for my life. Wave after wave of intense heat bombarded my face as the temperature climbed even higher, it felt like I was standing in front of an oven. Walter said nothing – and what was there to say really? The two of us stood in silence as the thing continued to creep closer to us.

The lights of my car fell flush on the Pastel Man's face now. That must have been what snapped Walter out of his trance. He made a break for his truck. The boy was fast, I'll give him that, but the hell beast leapt towards him with a surprising amount of speed and agility that I had not yet seen it demonstrate. Walter fell to the ground and tried to shuffle backwards in a futile effort to put distance between he and his devilish pursuer.

The guilt was swallowing me whole. I wanted nothing more than to wake up and find out that it was all a bad dream. It was Houston in the Summer time hot. Droplets of sweat dripped from my face to the ground below, sizzling on the asphalt before rising back into the air as puffs of steam. The sight of that thing as it lurked ever closer to the terrified boy was so dreadful that I turned my head in an effort to avert my eyes, but the Pastel Man made sure to remind me of our agreement.

"YOU MUST WATCH, YOUNG MAN! DON'T FORGET WE HAD A DEAL!"

I forced myself to peer back at the massacre that was about to take place. The creature's smile had mutated from mischievous to depraved. It looked as if it was deriving some sort of sick sexual pleasure from what it was about to put Walter through.

The Pastel Man grabbed Walter around his throat, easily hoisting the quarterback into the air with one arm. It stood there for a while, toying with him while forcing Walter to stare into those terrible pink eyes. After it had its fun, the creature reached into its satchel with its other hand, pulling out a much larger insect this time. It was different than the one it had forced my father to ingest, both in size and in appearance. If the bug I had seen it remove from its bag earlier that night was the size of a quarter then this one must have been as large as a golf ball. It was slimy too – the mucous like membrane that encased its body glistened in my cars headlights. The maggot like insect squirmed and shimmied between the creature's grimy fingers like a worm on a fishing hook. The Pastel Man teased the boy a bit longer, dangling the nasty bug in front of his face.

"Now be a good boy and open your mouth."

Walter screamed, which in retrospect was probably the worst thing he could have done. That gave the blue beast the opening it needed. It thrust the slimy insect in his mouth and past his tonsils with utter glee and elation. I watched on as Walter gagged on the oversized maggot as it made its way down his throat. It wasn't long before he began to lose color in his face and started choking. I desperately wanted to save him, but there was nothing I could do. A minute later and the Pastel Man dropped his lifeless body to the ground. It examined the carnage for a moment, as if it was pondering over a masterpiece in an art exhibit then shot a wide grin in my direction.

I could barely manage to speak, but I somehow managed to force out a few words, "You- you killed him."

The creature flared its nostrils again in satisfaction, but its face had become much more somber and serious. It wasn't sneering or scowling as I had seen it before when it lost its smile, instead it bore what I can only describe as a look of concern, like it was about to deliver some delicate news to me.

"Not without your help."

With that the demon turned away, retreating back towards the shadows and disappearing into the night without saying another word. I stood in the road, surveying the horrible scene. The frigid winter air returned back to the street that I was standing in, but even relief from the heat did little to soothe my distress.

Nothing had gone the way I had expected it to. I did not feel justified, or validated from the part I played in Walter's Death. The boy had not been eviscerated in some fantastical explosion. There was no brilliant light show ending in Walter's soul being dragged down to hell. There was just a dead boy in the road. A dead boy and his murderer. The Pastel

Man was the gun that he died by, but I was the one who pulled the trigger. In a way there were two dead boys in the road that evening.

I knew that I didn't have time to dawdle. At any moment a car could have come driving down the street and find me standing in the middle of that massacre. I sprinted back to my vehicle and sped down the road towards town. I'm not sure how much later the sun rose that morning. I couldn't bring myself to look.

The coroner attributed Walter's death to a drinking and driving accident, although there was understandably a lot of suspicion regarding the odd circumstances surrounding his demise. The autopsy revealed no evidence of the slimy bug that the Pastel Man had placed in Walter's throat. The town was devastated. I remember a candle light vigil was held in his honor. A couple of big news outlets even covered his death because of Walter's status as an elite college football recruit. But no one was more ravaged by his death than Mr. Flannigan. He fell into a deep depression. A year later, his marriage fell apart and his wife moved across the country. Understandably, he wasn't up for chitchat when I ran into him around town. I would still see him from time when visiting my friend, standing in his driveway holding a pigskin and pining over his fallen son – an empty husk of his former self, much like my soul that had been bled dry in the road that fateful evening.

***

My father made a full recovery and just a couple of days after his stroke was released from the hospital. I always had always appreciated the time we spent together, but after his near death I started to cherish every moment we shared.

I would go on to graduate high school and meet the love of my life the very first semester at my university. Your mother was the most beautiful girl I had ever seen and it didn't take much for me to fall head over heels for her. We married shortly after college. You were born not much later.

I was happy, Mathew. You and your mother helped me to forget about that night. No, forget isn't the right word. You helped me to ignore it. The shame was always there, but because my focus was directed towards providing a good life for the three of us there was little time to dwell on my past mistakes. In time, I had learned to bury those memories deeper and deeper inside of me until they almost didn't feel real anymore. For eight years you helped me find peace. Words cannot express how thankful I am for that.

Still, I feared that one day my serenity would end and the Pastel Man would show its terrible face to me once more so it could offer up another deal. Even on the eve of my father's passing, as I sat with your sleeping head resting on my shoulder in his hospital room, I was sure the Pastel Man would come. It did not and after that night, I started to believe that I was free of the creature. A weight had lifted from my chest, and even though I still carried the burden of my past deeds, life was going better than I could have ever dreamed. It was the type of thing that would make a man scoff at the concept of karma. After all, I had everything I ever wanted so why would such a wonderful life be afforded to someone who had committed such a terrible sin? But karma caught up with me, Mathew. Lord knows, karma caught up with me.

You were eight years old when it happened so I don't know how much you will remember about the accident by the time you read this letter. You and your mother were on your way back from the airport after visiting your grandparents. I was swamped at work and had to pull an all-nighter in order to finish a project by its deadline so Diana told me she would hail a taxi rather than ask me to pick the two of you up.

It was around midnight and I was alone in the office when I got a call from the police department. They told me a drunk driver had collided with your cab on the highway coming back from the airport. Your mother and the cabbie were killed on impact and I was told that you were in critical condition. I sat at my desk, unable to move or formulate a coherent thought. I remembered Mr. Flannigan and how he must have felt when the police informed him of Walter's death. I was so wrapped up in despair that I hadn't noticed how much warmer the room had gotten. Surprise struck me as I looked up to see the Pastel Man perched atop my boss' desk, that abhorrent smile once again painted across its nasty wrinkled face. It didn't need to speak or even make me an offer. This I believe the creature already knew.

"Can you save them?" I asked.

"Yes and no." it sang in a harmonious voice.

"What do you mean!? Just spit it out!"

The Pastel man's smirk disappeared and I could tell that it was not pleased with my tone. Memories of the vice grip it had on my face the last time I demanded something from the creature bled into my consciousness. But I was beyond the point of threats and perhaps it realized this because instead of lunging at me as the creature had done in the past, it decided to clarify its cryptic response.

"I cannot pull someone back from death's clutches, only save them before it grabs hold of them. Your wife is dead. Now make your peace with that. Your son's life on the other hand can be salvaged – for a price of course. You know the deal. Tit for tat."

I racked my mind. I couldn't think of a single person in my life who deserved to die at the hands of that pale blue monstrosity. Even Walter's bullying hadn't merited the gruesome death he suffered. How could I inflict that on yet another person? Then I thought about you, Mathew, clinging to life in a hospital bed. You didn't deserve to die either – not because *someone else* had made a poor decision that evening and got behind the wheel of a car when they were too intoxicated to drive. I wasn't going to let that happen lose your life.

The Pastel Man's glorious voice filled the room again. I seemed to be hearing it from all directions. "The drunk driver that crashed into your family's cab is still alive and in the very same hospital as your son. Why not him?"

For the first time that evening I looked into the large pink eyes of the creature. The heat had become unbearable. It felt as though my body was being held directly over a fire and I half expected my skin to begin blistering and bubbling over.

"You said it has to be someone I know?"

"Semantics. It just needs to be someone who has directly impacted your life. The moment he drove his car into your wife and son's taxi he became a candidate." The Pastel Man flared the tiny holes on its face with glee the way it always did when it was content with itself.

"Fine. Let's do it," I said. I shook its massive hand to make the arrangement official and The Pastel Man then gave me the instructions I needed to complete our deal.

When I met with the doctors at the hospital they updated me on your condition. "We've done all that we can, but he's a fighter," They feigned optimism, but I could see in their eyes that they didn't expect you to make it through the night.

They led me to your room so we could spend some time alone together. The Pastel Man was already there when I entered, smiling down on your broken body. Quickly I shut the door behind me and nodded to the creature. It reached a gangly arm into its satchel and pulled out the same type of colorful insect it had shoved down my father's throat. I opened your mouth and with two grubby fingers the creature crammed the bug deep into your oral cavity.

"He will make a full recovery," it said. "Now it's your turn."

The heat in the room began to dissipate as the Pastel Man disappeared behind the hospital curtain next to your bed. It was gone and I knew that if the creature showed itself again, then it would be because I spoke its name.

When I agreed to the bargain at my office The Pastel Man had told me what room the driver was being kept in. His injuries were far less severe than yours were so he was resting in a different wing of the facility.

I could feel my heart pounding as I made my way towards his room. With each step the beating in my chest grew more violent. Already the same guilt I had felt, looking down at Walter's corpse lying in the middle of the road began wash over me. Mr. Flannigan's heartbroken face occupied my thoughts. I felt just as ugly and horrible as the Pastel Man looked. I didn't have pointed teeth or wrinkly blue skin, but I wondered if going through with the deal made me a monster too.

I stepped as stealthily as possible through the door, hoping no one would notice me sneak in. As I looked down at the face of the driver lying unconscious in his bed, I instantly felt a familiar pang of regret. He was a boy, no older than Walter the night his life was snuffed out.

The driver was teenager – just a stupid teenager. One who made a horrible mistake. I saw Walter in the boy's face and my stomach began to churn. I wondered about who his loved ones were. Would his death crush them the same way my wife's death had crushed me? Would it tear apart their lives like Mr. Flannigan? I tried to call out the Pastel Man's name, but couldn't. The little angel on my shoulder wouldn't allow me. I decided then and there that I would not be responsible for the death of another boy. I would not pull the trigger. I walked out of his room and headed back to yours where I spent the rest of the evening sitting next to your bed and holding your hand.

The first few rays of morning sunlight that snuck into the hospital room caught my attention. I peeked out through the blinds and watched the sun rise for the first time since before the night Walter died. It was beautiful. The pink ribbon that lined the horizon had blended into the sky creating a dazzling purple hue. I had my light show, and it was spectacular.

I broke my deal with the Pastel Man and in doing so my fate now rests in its filthy hands. On the plus side, I know that you will recover from the accident. That's something that gives me great joy. I know it will be hard for you growing up without your parents, but you've always been close with your Aunt. She's a wonderful caring woman and promised us the day you were born that she would always be there if you needed her. Her husband, Benjamin, does well for himself and they've never had a problem with money. The life insurance policy Diana and I took out combined with the money we had been putting away for you to go to college will ensure that there should be no financial issues while you're under their care.

It's only a matter of time before the Pastel Man comes for me. I have accepted that my death is near, but I'm not scared. The room has already gotten unbearably hot and the humidity has made it much more difficult to breath. In a way I look forward to it. It's almost as if the boy that perished within me on that terrible night has been given another chance. When I die all the guilt and hate that I've had for myself over the years dies with me – wiped away so that my soul can cross over to a new plane of existence pure and innocent. The way it was before I ever met that monster.

One must die so another can live.

That's what the Pastel Man said.

Love Dad

Fast Enough

I run down the block – just as fast as my legs can possibly take me. And as I move into a full on sprint, so too does the beast. I think to myself that the sidewalk looks as though it must be ten miles long. It's amazing how the street of a seemingly ordinary residential neighborhood can transform into what feels like an endless stretch of road given the right circumstances. My heart is beating a million miles per hour and I don't know if it's from fatigue or panic. The demon, doubt, is screaming inside my head. It wants me to stop, to give up. It tells me there's no use in running, but I know I can't listen.

The dog is massive, 150lbs easy – a rabid blur of black matted fur, charging with the rage of a thousand nuclear blasts. As it snarls, mid gallop, I can see its horrible teeth. Teeth designed for ripping apart and tearing into flesh; teeth that it has every intention of using. It doesn't have the controlled, focused look of a predator. Instead its eyes are wild and ruthless. It wants to do more than kill; it wants to maim – inflict pain. I'm moving faster now than I've ever moved in my life. Terror is an unbelievable motivator.

There may be even more adrenaline pumping through my veins than blood at this point. My legs burn as lactic acid starts to flood my quadriceps and hamstrings like it's flowing from a broken levy. The muscles in my neck go tense. With every fiber of my being, I will myself to speed up even more, but deep down in the pit of my stomach, I know that I won't be fast enough. The dog is too quick and I'll never catch it. Not before it gets to my three-year-old son in the driveway.

The Ocean's Cool Air

I stared up and into the heavens. Stars dotted the evening sky like little white splotches of paint haphazardly splattered across a black canvas by some wannabe artist believing himself to be the second coming of Jackson Pollock. It reminded me of the type of piece one might find in a terrible, surrealist art gallery. One where pretentious hipsters sip Two-Buck Chuck out of plastic cups, all the while hoping their idiotic interpretations of each exhibit will make others think they're more intelligent than they actually are.

On a nearly moonless night the tiny twinkling specks of light were the only things illuminating the darkness brought on by dusk. I had grown to look forward to nightfall. The days had become unbearable due to the constant bombardment of UV rays that I had been forced to endure. The evening's cool air tended to my damaged skin and gave me reprieve from the daily beatings I took from the sun. The night also provided constellations, which had become a welcomed distraction. The stars told stories – stories that helped me forget – forget about the decrepit old lifeboat in the middle of the ocean that I was stranded in.

I barely noticed the commercial fishing boat as it approached my dinghy – a testament to how far-gone my mind had become from the weeks of isolation out at sea.

"Hey there! Are you ok?"

The young man was looking down at me from the bow of the ship. His piercing blue eyes almost glowed in contrast to the black sky behind him. I looked up at him; my sight had adapted to the darkness. I could see the whiskers that had begun to sprout from his face – a result of going days without shaving while out on the water. As he scratched his stubbly chin, more of the crew crowded around the front of the boat to take a gander at me. I suppose a half-dead man marooned out at sea was the strangest sight they'd seen in quite a while – an honor I would hold for only the briefest of moments.

"He's alive!" one of the fishermen shouted, "Let's get him up here now!"

As I watched the crew frantically buzz around the ship's deck like a bunch of worker bees, trying to figure out how to bring me aboard, a laugh escaped my mouth. Not a loud bellowing one, mind you, just a tiny giggle. It was the irony of the situation that I found comical. Perhaps that last little chuckle was the humor center of my brain finally fading from the weeks of emotional agony I had sustained. Going out not with a bang, but with a whimper – just a tiny giggle.

It started with a loud crash across the starboard side of their boat. The fishermen struggled to retain their footing when the powerful impact caused their vessel to rock onto its side, nearly capsizing it. Shouts and expletives streamed from the mouths of the startled sailors as I watched them desperately try to make sense of what had just occurred.

Another thunderous *CLANG* rang along the side of their ship and this time it tipped. The once silent ocean air was now filled with the sounds of chaos as the trawler smashed across the surface of the sea, flipping completely upside-down, and sending the men toppling overboard into the cold, murky water. I struggled to lift my head in order to peer over the side of my dinghy at the anarchy taking place around me.

The fishermen barely had a chance to breach and catch their breaths before it began pulling them back down into the abyss. Their panic quickly intensified as one by one, they started to realize their crewmates were disappearing into the deep, dark sea. You've never truly experienced pandemonium until you've heard a dozen grown men screaming for their lives in the middle of the ocean. The young man who had first greeted me from the ship's bow thrashed and kicked through the water, urgently trying to make his way towards my lifeboat. With salvation mere inches away, he flailed his arms wildly, reaching and grasping with reckless abandon, attempting to grab on to the side. I watched the hope in those piercing blue eyes of his turn to hopelessness as a black, sludge covered tentacle wrapped itself around his ankle and yanked him back down under with one quick jerk.

It was the fishing boat's turn now. Still sub-merged, the sea-beast easily crumpled the already twisted hunk of metal, before sinking it down to the watery graveyard at the bottom of the briny deep. There it would join countless other vessels that had shared a similar fate.

Without warning, the massive creature erupted from the surface of the sea. I wondered briefly if the salty taste of the water that splashed my face when the beast made its appearance stemmed the ocean itself or the blood of the men who had died in it. I shut my eyes, hoping not to catch a glimpse of its horrible features. The sound of water trickling around the leviathan's body as it waded towards my lifeboat caused me to wince in fear. Though my eyes were clenched tight, I could still feel its awful presence as it closed in on me. I gagged and choked as the rancid smell of its hot breath forced its way into my nostrils and down my throat. With a *thud*, it dropped a mangled human limb across my lap – one of the fishermen's arms to be precise.

It spoke only one word. The same word it had said to me many times before and the same word it would repeat many times after.

"*Eat.*"

And with that it slithered back into the sea, leaving me to myself again. I opened my eyes and stared down at the mutilated piece of flesh lying across my sunburnt thighs. For a moment I was tempted to throw it back overboard, but thought the better of it, fearing retaliation from the creature for not listening to its commands. For whatever reason, it seemed to want me alive, but I wasn't about to test its patience. I sunk my teeth into the skin and tore a chunk of muscle from the bone. It had been a week since I had last eaten. The hunger pains in my stomach helped to subdue the horrors in my mind and made the atrocity of cannibalism slightly easier.

I let out a sigh and looked back up to the starry night. I was alone again, and once more only silence reigned over the ocean's cool air.

The Wendall Lane Diaries: You Shouldn't

Disclaimer: I am not a paranormal investigator. I am an author. While looking for inspiration for a book, I came across a series of stories surrounding a home in the American Pacific North West. It is an extremely ordinary looking house in an extremely ordinary looking residential neighborhood, but the stories that have emanated from its former residents and the people who lived in the town that it's located in are quite extraordinary.

Through my research of the house on Wendall Lane, I have come across accounts that range from the super natural to just plain bizarre. In order to protect the privacy of the people in the town and the current inhabitants of the house on Wendall Lane, I have not only changed the name of everyone in these stories, but the name of the street as well. Wendall Lane is just an alias for the true location of these accounts.

***

Alan Palmer lived in the house on Wendell Ln. from September 2002 to July 2003. After months of trying to contact him about his time there, I finally received an e-mail agreeing to set up a meeting. Quite a few of the house's prior residents had turned down my requests for face to face interviews so I jumped at the chance to talk to him in person once the opportunity presented itself.

Palmer, who worked as a socioeconomics professor at the University of Washington, arranged to meet me and talk over drinks at a place of his choosing in downtown Seattle. The bar was called Oliver's Lounge and was located in the historic Mayflower Park Hotel. Upon arriving, I was surprised to see just how crowded it was for 3:00 PM on a Tuesday. There were people seated at nearly every table while food runners and waiters dressed in white servers' jackets and black bowties hustled and bustled about the room bringing people their orders. Windows stretching from floor to ceiling allowed for an ample amount of sunlight to illuminate the space, giving it a genuinely open and inviting ambience. I spotted Palmer in the corner sitting at a small high table and sipping on a glass of scotch.

He greeted me with a hearty handshake and a bright smile after I introduced myself to him. The man was greying a little around the ears, and I could tell shortly after meeting him that he was incredibly intelligent, but aside from that he seemed to have the demeanor of a fellow 15 years his junior. Palmer was a light-hearted gentleman who loved a good joke and he insisted on telling me a few of his favorites before I turned my tape recorder on.

Once he had his fun we started the interview.

Believe it or not, you're not the first person who's tried to contact me about the time I spent living on

Wendell Ln. Apparently there are all kinds of "ghost enthusiasts" out there who've heard about the house through the various online forums these types of people tend to frequent. Nerds and losers – you know the type – they spend their time sifting through thread after thread on the Internet, pretending that they're doing something productive with their lives. Hell, most of them are probably overweight man-children sitting in their parents' basement and conducting their "research" in between anime cartoons.

Palmer let out a laugh, seemingly pleased with his depiction of the paranormal research community. I decided to omit the fact that I first heard about him through one of the online forums he was talking about. He took a sip of scotch and continued on.

So naturally I ignored your e-mails thinking you were another one of those ghost geeks. It's strange. I probably wouldn't have agreed to meet, but I came across one of your books by complete accident. My nephew mentioned your work in passing when I was over at my brother's house for dinner a few weeks ago. I put two and two together and realized you were the same author who had been e-mailing me so I figured why the hell not? I'm game to talk about it if you are, all though I must admit my story probably isn't as interesting as demons or monsters or whatever the hell it is you write about. Not a whole lot happened while I was living there. In fact, the only reason I lived in the house for such a short period of time was because an old colleague of mine offered me a full professorship here at the University of Washington not long after I purchased it and the commute was just too far. My workplace at the time had no job security, I was on the chopping block every year so there was no way I could turn down the offer. This was before the housing bust in '07. It was a sellers' market; banks were giving away loans like there was no tomorrow so it wasn't difficult to turn right back around and flip the place. Hell, I even made thirty grand! Plus, I love Seattle. The weather sucks, but this city has culture!

We made small talk for a bit. He told some stories about work, his travels to Europe, and even asked me about some of the upcoming books that I've been working on. I was beginning to wonder if flying all the way out to Seattle to speak to him had been a big waste of time. After all, Palmer appeared almost completely uninterested in discussing any and all aspects of the house. I directed his attention back towards the reason why we had met when I asked him to describe the most bizarre encounter he could remember having in the short time he lived on Wendell Ln.

Haha! Now you're starting to sound like the Internet ghost geeks! Fine, fine, let me think. Like I said, nothing really strange ever happened, that's why I –

He paused for a moment and looked out the window towards the street.

There was one thing. I had almost forgotten about it – the TV incident. It was a Friday night in June, about a month before the house sold. There was nothing on. You know how crappy television programming can be on the weekends, especially in the summer time! I was scrolling through channels on my TV's menu looking for something to turn my brain off to when the title of a show caught my eye. It was called "You Shouldn't Watch". I figured with a name like that, how could I not give it a go? Also, the show was on a channel I had never seen before – Channel 732. To be honest, I don't watch much TV and when I do, I don't usually venture out of the HD channels so I wasn't even sure if it was covered under my cable package.

Now, I don't know what yours looks like, but the way my cable provider's menu was set up, different colors were used to distinguish between different types of shows. You'd get green for sports, purple for movies, and blue for everything else. However, the menu color for this particular show was black. The text was yellow, which was also unusual since the show's title is always written in white. Even the font was different. Don't ask me to describe what it looked like because I really can't recall. All I know was I had never seen letters written in that way before. I know that sounds odd, but the best description I could give you is that even though the lettering looked completely alien in appearance, my mind could somehow interpret what it said – "YOU SHOULDN'T WATCH". Now I'm starting to sound like the Internet weirdos. Ha!

Palmer polished off his glass and called the waitress over to order another drink.

Anyways, from the very second I turned on the program, I knew I was watching something very strange – very strange indeed. The black and white picture on my television was of a mostly empty room. There were no visible windows or doors; the place seemed cold and uninviting – like how I'd imagine a jail cell in Bangladesh would look. Not dead center, but slightly off to the left of the frame was a man sitting at an old rusty table. He was shirtless and looked to be very malnourished. It reminded me of those old photos you see of the Jews who suffered through German concentration camps during World War 2. I remember wondering if he was a prisoner there. The frail man wore a pair of tattered slacks, but no belt or shoes. His mouth hung a gape as if his jaw was too heavy to close. There was no music or dialogue; the only noises radiating from my speakers were the sounds of his wheezy, raspy breaths. God! It sounded like he was suffering from emphysema or something. I followed his gaze down to an old rotary phone sitting on the tabletop. He just gawked at the thing like a buffoon while I stared at the screen, mesmerized by the odd scene taking place on my television.

I hit the info button, hoping to read a synopsis of what the show was about, but of course there was nothing so I just kept watching. For minutes he didn't move. I giggled to myself for a bit – you know, the way you do when something makes you uncomfortable and your brain thinks laughing will ease the tension. The whole time I was waiting, hoping for something that resembled dialogue. Anything to prove that I was just watching some weird movie and had simply turned it on at the wrong time, but nothing ever happened. Perplexed and a little bit bored, I stood up from my couch and headed over to the kitchen to rummage through the fridge for a little late night snack. I was about halfway done making myself a sandwich when I heard the most terrible noise.

Palmer paused briefly. At first I thought he had stopped his story because of the waitress returning from the bar with his drink, but he barely acknowledged her presence. The man was caught up in deep thought as though he had just remembered something important. When he finally began speaking again the tone of his voice had completely changed. Gone was the chipper upbeat persona I had come to know him by. Palmer was clearly distraught.

It sounded horrible – like a dying animal. I remember an awful sensation of nausea washing over me; it was the strangest thing. There was an ominous feeling in the air too – death, ruin, calamity all hanging over my head. Once I realized that the noise was coming from the television, I put down my sandwich and hurried back towards the living room. The scene on the TV was essentially the same except now the sickly looking man had turned his head up towards the ceiling and was howling and groaning in the most unpleasant of ways. The longer I watched the more it made me feel like I was going to retch. The whole thing was utterly abhorrent. The man would moan for 30 maybe 40 seconds at a time before stopping suddenly, then he would take another deep wheezy breath and the terrible sounds would begin anew. I cringed as I took it all in. My visual and auditory senses were being assaulted by the most disagreeable of stimuli and I was still fighting off the urge to vomit all over my living room carpet. Just when I thought things couldn't get worse, the man still groaning mind you, turned his head in the direction of the screen and stared straight into the camera. The thing is, I was certain he was looking directly at me. That's what it felt like; it was almost as if we were in the same room. I probably should have turned off the show, but after minutes of nothing something was finally going on and I felt compelled to keep watching even though I was suffering immensely.

I stared into the glazed over eyes of the sickly looking man until he turned his attention down towards the phone sitting on the table –

Palmer hunched over in his seat and removed his glasses. He seemed visibly shaken. The 42-year-old econ professor clasped the bridge of his nose between his thumb and index finger and let out a deep sigh. Beads of sweat had begun to form on his forehead.

I'm sorry, forgive me. I haven't thought about this night in a long time. I suppose it's possible that my mind pushed this episode to the back of my consciousness and I forgot all about it – kind of a defense mechanism type of thing. I've read about case studies where army veterans who witnessed horrific events develop amnesia about their time in the military. It seems as though I may be going through something similar, except as I sit here and talk to you, everything begins to come back to me.

I asked him if he wanted to continue. He agreed and then resumed his story.

His hand quaked violently as he lifted the phone to his ear. His arms were rail thin and it looked as though he was struggling mightily to hold it in place. With his other hand, he clumsily started spinning the rotary dial. That's when my cell phone started ringing.

A chill ran down my spine, my nausea got even worse, that ominous feeling in the air had transformed into full on horror. I prayed with every fiber in my being that it was a coincidence as I looked at my phone's caller ID. You have no idea how bad I wanted the number to be one that I recognized. I didn't recognize it of course. Hell, it wasn't even a number. It was something else entirely. `In that same strange, alien text from the TV's menu were the words "YOU SHOULDN'T LISTEN" written where the caller's number should have been.

That was enough for me. I hung up the phone and reached for the remote on the coffee table. I must have pressed the channel button a dozen times, but the picture never changed. I tried the power button and still nothing happened. The man began to dial the phone again. Once more my cell started to ring.

Palmer had gone pale. He looked completely different from when I first met him – the polar opposite of the smiling man who shook my hand earlier.

I tried to turn off the TV manually, I even unplugged it from the wall, but by this time I knew it would do nothing. The sickly, pale man continued to stare at me – his horrible, empty gaze felt as though it was tearing me to pieces. Stomach bile slowly started to crawl its way up my esophagus. I don't know why I answered the phone, I couldn't help myself; maybe I thought if I did then it would all just end. My finger trembled as I pressed the answer button. I slowly lifted the phone to my face.

I didn't even need to say, "hello". He just began speaking as if he was watching me answer the phone through the television screen – and perhaps he was.

Tears began to well up in Palmer's eyes. I tried to tell him that he didn't need to go into further detail if he was uncomfortable, but he kept talking as though he never even heard me. By that point, he would have finished his story even if there was no one sitting across the table from him.

He spoke to me in a terrible voice – it sounded like he was gargling shards of glass. His lips moved on the screen, but I could hear him clearly over the phone... he said...he said, "You shouldn't tell". Then in one horrible, inhumanly quick motion, he leapt out of the frame as the screen went to black.

Jesus Christ, he said, "You shouldn't tell." Did I just tell? Vincent please, does that mean I just told!?"

Palmer fell silent and stared awkwardly into his glass for a moment. Then he apologized and excused himself from the table. It was the last I saw of him that night. He sent me a text message 15 minutes later explaining that he had to go home and instructing me to charge the bill to his tab. I tried to contact him once I got back to California, but he never answered my calls or e-mails. A few weeks later I found out what happened to him after performing a simple Google search of his name.

Twelve days after Alan Palmer and I met to talk about the house on Wendall Ln, he was found dead in his Seattle home. There was no sign of a struggle or forced entry, however, due to the horrific nature of his death, Seattle PD does believe that he was murdered.

Palmer's body was discovered in front of the television on his living room couch missing ears, eyes, and tongue.

Love Hurts

I met her in a hotel bar. I was just some lonely sap looking down at the bottom of an empty glass. Three Side Car's deep and I was feeling a little tipsy, but I still had my wits about me. I spotted her eyeing me from across the room. She was gorgeous. You should have seen her. This gal had fire engine red hair, emerald green eyes, and a body that just wouldn't quit. A woman like that could have any man she wanted. I didn't know what it was she possibly saw in a guy like me, but I sure as hell wasn't going to complain.

She made her way over to me and ordered a drink – a Lemon Drop I think it was. We got to chatting, she told me her name; I told her a few jokes. She chuckled at them, but now that I think about it, she probably would have laughed at anything to get me upstairs.

We headed up to my room for a nightcap. The red headed seductress made me one more drink from the mini bar before things started getting hot and heavy. I think I fell in love with her right then and there. Her lips were so soft. They felt amazing as she pressed them against my neck. That's the last thing I remember before everything went black.

When I opened my eyes I was lying naked in the bathtub. Blood was gushing from a freshly opened gaping hole in my body like a geyser. That's when I saw her. She walked into the bathroom carrying an icebox and a surgical kit, still looking as radiant and beautiful as ever. When she noticed that I was alert and cognizant, her face went white. I'll never forget her scream as she ran from my hotel room and out of my life.

It took years to get over that night. I still think about her from time to time. Love hurts, you know? I gave her my heart. I guess it just kind of freaked her out that I was still alive after she removed it.

Brownstone

The large brownstone apartment building I used to live in was mostly empty. The only other tenants were a nice elderly lady on the first floor named Doris, and a young couple who lived across the hall from me on the second floor. Coincidentally, their apartment was directly above Doris'. I didn't mind the young couple, but I found them to be a bit anti-social. They pretty much kept to themselves, barely acknowledging me when I passed them in the hall or ran into them in the laundry room. Every now and then the young man would give me a head nod, but even that was a rarity. The thing that did bother me about them was the constant arguing I would frequently hear coming from their apartment. Shouts and cries would echo through the building's hallways, carrying all the way into my bedroom – sometimes in the dead of night.

Over the winter months, as a blanket of snow fell over the city, the young couple's arguments began to get worse. Often I found myself lying in bed, covering my ears in an attempt to drown out the sound of the man's voice as he viciously berated his young lover. Even the quieter evenings were not without the occasional boom of a fist colliding with a wall or the crash of shattered glass. It was the day after one of these particularly nasty arguments that I noticed a black eye on the young woman as I passed her in the hall. When I asked her if her boyfriend had hit her she broke down in my arms, sobbing uncontrollably.

I took her into my apartment to ask some follow up questions and make her some hot tea, but once inside, I barely had time to boil some water before she threw herself at me and gave me the most passionate kiss of my entire life.

We made love right there, on my kitchen table. Even with her swollen eye I still found her beautiful. We held each other for what felt like an eternity before the banging started on my door. It was her boyfriend and he didn't sound pleased. I told him to get lost or I would call the cops and report him, which was something I still planned on doing anyways. Eventually, after an hour long standoff, he gave up and retreated back to his apartment. I never even asked the young woman her name. We just lied in bed, laughing and talking in each other's arms, before falling asleep. When I awoke in the morning she was gone.

Of course I was upset. I had developed strong feelings for her, but I was more concerned for her safety than anything else. I had no idea what her boyfriend would do to her if she went back and told him about what happened between us. I slipped into some jeans, ran across the hall, and started knocking on their door to check in on her. My knocks were met with only silence. I put my ear to the door in hopes that I could hear voices, a television, anything, but there was no noise.

Later that day I stopped by Doris' on my way out of the building and asked her if she had heard anything going on in the apartment above her earlier that morning. She looked at me like I was crazy when I mentioned the couple and how I was genuinely worried for the young woman. Doris mockingly placed the back of her hand to my forehead as if she was checking for a fever. She went on to inform me that no one lived above her and we were the only two tenants in the building.

I called the landlord and told him about the young couple, but he insisted that the apartment had not been rented. Just in case, he decided to come down later that day and open it up in order to make sure the couple I described weren't squatters. He arrived to the building at around three in the afternoon. I pointed out the apartment to him that the young couple lived in, but when he opened the door the place looked like it hadn't inhabited in years. There was no furniture and a thick layer of dust coated the floor. The landlord gave me an irritated look and asked me why I was wasting his time, but all I could do was stand in the barren room wide-eyed and slack jawed.

If you think that this story ends with the couple disappearing, never to be heard from again then you are wrong. Later that evening a loud commotion rumbled from the mysterious apartment. The sound of the young woman's wails tore through the air like a buzz saw. Even from behind the door I could hear her boyfriend's palm as it struck the soft cheeks I had been kissing just the night before. I tried to force my way in, but the heavy oak door wouldn't budge when I rammed my shoulder into it. I called the police, but the ruckus subsided before they arrived. Needless to say, they weren't too pleased once they finally got the door open only to find the unit unoccupied.

However, as the months rolled along and the snow melted away, the arguments continued on. Doris never heard the screams and shouts above her even though the fights had gotten louder and were carrying on longer than ever. I called the police a couple more times. Each visit they found the apartment completely empty. I eventually stopped when they started threatening to take legal action. But the fighting did not.

Every once in a while I would still see the young woman in the hall, always looking down to avoid eye contact with me as she passed by. Not once would she answer my questions when I tried to speak to her. Even more disturbing was the state her face had become – more battered and bruised each time I saw her. After a while both eyes had become swollen shut and puffy like a prizefighter's immediately after a hard fought bout. Black and purple bruises covered almost every inch of her skin and she wore the outlines of her boyfriend's fingers around her throat like a necklace. The bridge of the young woman's once straight nose had become crooked and zigzagged off in multiple directions.

Her boyfriend on the other hand, just stared at me with the most disdainful eyes every time I'd see him. He too would remain silent when I tried to ask him questions or threaten to have him arrested. I wanted to hit him, but unprovoked violence is against my ethical code. Besides, had I struck him, he would surely take his anger out on her.

On top of it all, I was beginning to doubt my sanity. I could hear the couple, see the couple, I even felt the young woman's touch, but every time I demanded to be let into their apartment, either by the police or the landlord, it was just as empty and dusty as the first time I had seen it. Still the fighting in the apartment across the hall never ceased.

I finally decided that the environment was too toxic for me to deal with so I decided to move to a newer, more modern building on the East Side. I hoped to put the awful experiences from the brownstone behind me, but unfortunately this was not the case. Not a day passes by where I don't catch a glimpse of them. I see the couple when I get off the elevator, exit my car in the parking lot, or walk alone down the hall at night.

Her face is more twisted and contorted than ever – so smashed and swollen that it could not even pass for human anymore. Her head dangles haphazardly off to the side, as if her neck was no longer capable of supporting its weight. Puss oozes from open sores on the young woman's arms, legs, and face, while yellow bile dribbles from her mouth, down the front of her chest. Scar tissue has formed over half of her scalp where her beautiful golden hair used to be. And perhaps worst of all, those supple lips, that once felt so soft and comforting as they pressed against mine appeared to have been torn clean off her face, exposing a set of jagged teeth jutting out from her bleeding, swollen gums. And he just stares at me through those hateful eyes as the two of them follow me down the hallway and all the way to my apartment door.

Sweet Talk

"I love you," she said. Hearing her talk like that made me feel all warm and fuzzy on the inside. "You know," she bit her bottom lip. The naughtiest little glimmer danced in her eye. *"I can't get you out of my head."*

"I can't get you out of my head, either," I whispered. Just being around her made me so nervous.

She giggled. "Alright then, goodnight. Call me in the morning. I can't wait to hear your voice again."

"Goodnight," is what I think her boyfriend said on the other end of the line.

She hung up the phone.

That's when I opened up the door of the closet I had been hiding in, making sure to block off the exit of her bedroom. I pulled a roll of duct tape from my jacket pocket...

Little Black Bugs

It's important you understand that I'm not insane. I say this because the tale I'm about to recount may seem preposterous – outlandish even! So bizarre that if you didn't know better, you'd think you were reading the words of a madman. Nevertheless, I assure you this narrative only contains the unequivocal truth about what happened to me – *about how my life brought me to this.*

I'm afraid that I must write quickly though. I wish to tell you the whole story, but unfortunately I'll have to omit some details due to the time constraints that are being placed upon me this evening. The guests at my door are growing restless and if I don't write this confession in a swift, prompt manner then I fear I won't get the chance to finish it. It is for that reason that I am apologizing in advance for giving you the abbreviated version of my account. You see? A loon would never feel remorse for such a thing!

My story began six weeks ago. I had just moved into my brother's apartment – the very one I'm composing my tale from this evening. I use the term "brother" loosely because that's the type of designation one might typically employ to describe another human being. Donald was more of a pig than a person – a slovenly, fat oaf who did nothing but sit around in his shit-stained underwear, smoke weed, fart, and eat junk food all day. Everything about him made me sick – from the greasy, curly hair that sat on top of his blubbery head, all the way down to the crusty unkempt toenails I would often catch him nonchalantly picking at on the sofa. You should have seen the way he mined the dirt and grime that settled under those claws of his, only stopping to flick his nasty toe-filth to the carpet below or to wipe it on the couch's cushion with his crud covered fingers. Things like that often made me wonder how it was even physically possible that the same two people sired us. I would have assumed either he or I to be adopted, but unfortunately, if you looked past his pimples, greasy skin, and stretch marks, it was obvious that we bore far too much of a resemblance to each other not to be related.

It was my first year at college. Donald was a junior, though I'd barely call him a student since he rarely went to class and was hanging on to a C average by the skin of his teeth. My parents had decided that it would be best for us to room together while we were both in school. The living arrangement saved them money since they wouldn't need to pay for two apartments and I think they hoped that my studious, tidy habits would rub off on my older brother.

The apartment was located in student housing off campus. The building held about 40 units, all of which were inhabited by students at the university. I of course, being the social butterfly that I am, decided to introduce myself and make friends with many of the buildings tenants. This is a completely rational, non-crazy thing for a person who just moved into a new building to do, don't you think?

As I went door to door, shaking hands with each of my new neighbors, it became increasingly more evident that the building had a strong community atmosphere. Many of the students knew each other and I found out there were regular soirees and get-togethers in order to help the newbies like myself mingle and make friends. I was having a great time meeting new people and everyone seemed to be genuinely inviting. Of all the students in my building that I met that day, it was Elizabeth in apartment 303 whom I liked the best. She was a beautiful girl with a sweet and charming demeanor. I like to think of myself as somewhat smooth, but I must admit, I was at a loss for words when she answered the door. It was her gorgeous green eyes that caught me off guard. They were absolutely stunning, like she was looking out at me through a pair of brilliant, gleaming emeralds. Her hair was equally as breathtaking – a dazzling auburn red she wore knotted into a French braid that dangled carelessly over her shoulder, lightly caressing her bosom. *Oh how I longed to be that braid!* If that wasn't enough, she was intelligent too. Elizabeth was in her second year of school, studying biochemistry – by no means an easy subject. She even had aspirations of going to graduate school and becoming a PhD – not just one of those pretty girls who gets by on her looks! *No sir!*

Some of the other neighbors I talked with were surprised to find out that I was not only rooming with, but also related to my disgusting older brother. A few of them even shared horror stories about the foul stench they would sometimes encounter when they accidently passed too close to his apartment door on the way to the laundry room. Others joked about the stomach turning sights they had caught glimpses of on those rare occasions Donald opened the blinds of his windows to let sunlight into his unit. I felt a great deal of shame and embarrassment listening to their anecdotes – not just for my brother, but for myself as well. It was a curse to be related to such a revolting troll!

As bad as the other tenants assumed Donald's apartment to be, I'm certain no one really had any idea just how terrible it actually was. I don't think I could have ever shown my face around that building again if they knew the truth. When I moved in, the apartment was one of the most repulsive places I had ever had the displeasure of laying my eyes upon. Donald lived alone before I became his roommate so for two years there was no one cleaning up after his over-weight, unrefined ass.

Trash bags full of fast food wrappers and stale, half-eaten pizza crust laid strewn about the living room, producing a smell akin to that of a hobo defecating in a McDonald's dumpster on a hot day. The fridge in the kitchen was filled with rotten meat, moldy fruit (that I'm sure he never touched), and multiple containers of Tupperware, each occupied by a different putrid, soupy substance that resembled the habitat of an alien world more than something you could eat for lunch.

The bathroom was even more repulsive and sickening than any port-a-john you might come across at a summer music festival. The inside of the once white toilet bowl had been stained a deep orange from the years of abuse at the hands, or rather, ass of my brother. Not once had he considered cleaning away the sludge that had collected along the walls of the pot. Tiny brown bits of fecal matter even sprinkled the seat itself! *How do you get shit on the seat!?* Given Donald's repugnant nature, I might have understood if it was just the toilet, but the shower and sink were equally as mucky. The drains of both were clogged with coarse black curly hair and some sort of thick yellow goop that looked as though it might have been radioactive.

Then there was his bedroom. *Oh God, his bedroom!* Just thinking about the way it looked that first day makes me shudder. Where shall I start? Well, for one, there were the plastic solo cups sitting on his nightstand and windowsill filled to the brim with urine.

"I'm just too tired to get up and walk to the bathroom in the middle of the night." He would later explain to me. "That's why I always keep a 'piss cup' near by. You know? In case nature calls." Why he never thought to empty them out, I have no idea.

I found used wads of tissue paper, soaked in what I can only assume to be the special ingredient one might use to create horrible, miniature pig-babies, scattered around his room like some sort of terrible

Easter Egg hunt from Hell. His clothes were everywhere. I'm not sure if the human bag of waste had ever heard of a closet, but I'm fairly positive the concept of a washing machine was completely foreign to him because every t-shirt or pair of socks I picked up off the floor stunk worse than George "The Animal" Steele's jock strap after wrestling a 45 minute "slobbernocker" in Madison Square Garden.

My living conditions were unfit for a barnyard animal and desperately needed to be addressed. Some of the people I met from the building (Elizabeth included) had invited me to a start-of-the-school-year BBQ. As much fun as it sounded, I was forced to decline due to enormous amount of cleaning I had ahead of me. The last thing I wanted to do was return to that nauseating place with a belly full of red meat and beer. If I did, I can promise you one thing, *my belly wouldn't stay full for long!*

I first noticed the insects that night when I was tidying up the kitchen. It was around a quarter past eight and I had just set about cleansing and disinfecting the fridge. I was dumping the last container of primordial soup down the garbage disposal when I felt a little *prick* on the nape of my neck. This triggered a knee jerk reaction, causing me to reach back and grasp wildly at the source of my irritation. To my surprise, when I brought my hand back from behind my neck, I realized I had caught something between my fingers – a little black bug, no bigger than a millimeter in diameter. Its body was round, similar to that of a ladybug. Two long antennas protruded from its head. It wasn't dead yet; I had crushed it's body, but its legs were still moving in a fruitless attempt to escape. I didn't get more than a quick glance at the pesky thing before another one scurried by me on the kitchen counter. One swat of my hand later and both the little buggers were dead. I believed them to be pantry pests, like a rice weevil or something of that sort, though in time I would come to discover that this theory was wrong. *Lord knows how wrong I was!*

Naturally, Donald was of little use when it came to cleaning. I worked tirelessly just to keep the apartment livable while he would completely undo everything by the time I got back form school. As the weeks wore on, I started to realize I was fighting a losing battle. The good days were the ones where I could maintain equilibrium and go to sleep with the apartment looking no more dingy then when I woke up that morning, but I never cleaned fast enough to gain any ground on the chaos and clutter my brother created. While I scrubbed and scoured away at the stains on the carpet or threw load after load of his dirty unmentionables in the washer he would already be busy constructing another mountain of garbage for me to clean up. It was around this time that I began to develop genuine feelings of hatred for Donald.

Those bothersome bugs had become a constant reminder of the filth I was living in. I'd usually see them one or two at a time, sometimes congregating in the bathroom, trying to get into my tube of toothpaste or crawling along the top of cereal boxes in the cupboard. On occasion, I would feel that familiar *prick* on my arms or legs and look down to find the nasty little vermin feeding on me. I had never lived in a home with pests before, but I was no fool. There were more of them, hiding behind the walls. I was sure of it. *Where there's one there's a million.* That's what they say about infestations. The thought of a thin layer of stucco being the only thing separating me from that army of insects made me tremble on more than one occasion. It frustrated me to know that it was my brother's bad habits that had most likely attracted them there in the first place.

I would often daydream about inviting Elizabeth over to hang out, watch TV, and well...do other things, but I knew that as long as my pest-ridden apartment continued to be treated like a garbage dump, our relationship could only remain a fantasy. *How humiliating it would be if she saw how I was living!* I was far too embarrassed to get close to her and I had my brother to thank for that.

***

Blast! Those idiots knocking at my door are nothing if not persistent. I keep telling them that I need more time, but it's clear that they've become impatient with my stalling. I might as well skip to the important part of the story then.

Things went from bad to worse the day I ran into Chuck Volderschmidt while he was smoking a cigarette down by the dumpster behind my building. Chuck was a simple fellow, a second year senior only slightly brighter than my brother. He was one of the few residents of my apartment complex other than Donald whom I had developed a strong distaste for in my short time living there. Maybe it was because he was the type of guy who majored in woman's studies and took poetry as an elective because it was "a good place to meet dumb broads". The guy had all the honor and integrity of a used car salesman and it wasn't hard to picture him twenty years from now working as a clerk behind the desk of a porn shop, balding and sporting the kind of pencil thin mustache you only see on child molesters. I had just finished tossing away a garbage bag full of Donald's "love tissues" (which I had found all over his bedroom following one of his infamous all-day marathon sessions) when Chuck finally decided to acknowledge my presence.

"Sup man?" he said in the most comically detached, *too cool to care* voice I've ever heard. "What've you been up to? You missed a great party in 412 last week."

"I've been busy with school, Chuck." That wasn't a lie. Acting as Donald's live in maid afforded me little time to study. I was spending my down time catching up with my classes. I continued on. "I know I haven't been around all that much, it's just that –"

"Hey check this out, man." He cut me off. Of course he was only interested in sparking up a conversation because he wanted to brag about something. "You know Elizabeth in 303, right?"

I raised an eyebrow. "Yeah. What about her?"

"I totally finger banged her in Jessica Brakowtzki's bathroom at the party!"

"I don't believe you." I didn't.

"Seriously, man! Here, smell," he lifted his finger to my face. I swatted it away. He giggled like an idiot while I silently talked myself down from cracking his skull open on the pavement.

"Yeah man. I've been hittn' it for a week now. She's totally in to me too. Best part is, I don't even need to buy her dinner or nothn'. She just comes over and I smash that ass 'till the sun comes up."

It took every ounce of my energy not run my fist into the shit-eating grin on his face. I knew he wasn't trying to annoy me; he was just a moron. Chuck didn't know about my feelings for Elizabeth and I'm sure if he did, the little coward wouldn't have dreamed about saying those things to me.

"Cool, man. Good for you," I said.

I brushed past the smarmy boob on my way back into the building and proceeded up the stairs towards Elizabeth's apartment. If Chuck was telling people lies about her then she deserved to know. My heart started to beat emphatically in my chest as I neared closer to her door. When I arrived, I knocked, then cupped my palm over my mouth once I heard her footsteps approaching, exhaling into my hand in order to make sure my breath was pleasant. It smelled exquisitely minty and fresh – as per usual. Elizabeth answered the door wearing the cutest pair of pink shorts and a workout top.

"Oh hi," I said, slightly taken aback by the sight of her silky smooth legs. "I, uh…" and suddenly I didn't care about Chuck Voldershmidt anymore. All I wanted was to place my arms around her lovely waist and run my fingers along her elegant curves. It was now or never. I had decided to finally man up and ask her out. I didn't care about her seeing my apartment anymore. Surely an angel like that would understand my plight. Maybe if things went well between us, I could even move out of my brother's place and in with Elizabeth.

She stood leaning against the doorframe, watching me with a perplexed look on her face, probably wondering why I had shown up at her apartment.

"What's up?" she asked me.

"Elizabeth..." I stuttered. "I...um...I was wondering if...if you'd like to grab a bite to eat sometime?"

She smiled (*The most enchanting smile I've ever seen!*) and looked out at me with those sexy green eyes of hers before uttering a dispiriting string of words that ground my heart into powder and scattered its remains into the wind.

"I'd love to, but I'm actually already kind of seeing Chuck Volderschmidt. You know him right?"

Chuck Volderschmidt. Chuck "No Means Yes, Captain Fingerbang, Fucking" Volderschmidt! It isn't even fathomable how a woman like Elizabeth could find herself interested in a guy like him. Yet somehow, as ridiculous and unlikely as it sounded, that was precisely what she had told me. I don't remember what I said to her after that or how pathetic I looked as I slinked away from her door. All I do remember is that I ended up shuffling back to my apartment in a depressed haze with my tail tucked between my legs.

Of course Donald was asleep on the couch by the time I came back. When I had left he had been laying in the same position watching TV, one hand in his pants cupping his balls, the other pinching the roach end of a joint. The place looked like hell. In the time I was gone, he had managed to knock over the glass of Hawaiian Punch that was sitting on the coffee table, creating a large red stain on the carpet and leaving the living room looking like a crime scene. During his siesta, he dropped the still burning roach on the rug and was lucky he hadn't started a fire. I shook my head in disgust as I picked it up off the floor.

I decided a bit of busywork would help to take my mind off of Elizabeth and Chuck so I began cleaning. Donald's bedroom was a good place to start. There was always something in there that reeked so bad it could make a man forget his own name so I grabbed a trash bag and made my way into the pigpen.

My bag was about halfway filled with soda cans when I came across a pizza box from a local restaurant called Fat Sal's sitting next to Donald's industrial size tube of "hand" lotion on the floor. I recognized the box. Donald ordered pizza from that place at least a couple times a week. He and the delivery guy even seemed to be on a first name basis. On the box's lid, an over-weight Italian American stereotype in a chef's hat was pictured. One hand rested on his pudgy hip while the other extended a thumb into the air to go along with the portly chef's approving smile. There was no slogan written on the box, but I came up with an appropriate one in my head.

So what if my food takes years off your life and gives you a worse complexion than The Toxic Avenger? At least it tastes good! -Fat Sal

It was only morbid curiosity that motivated me to lift the lid. I was interested to know what it was about the place that made Donald prefer it to the fifty thousand other pizza restaurants around campus. Perhaps I should have been better prepared for what I was about to see. After all, I'd surmise that a few weeks of cleaning Donald's disaster of a room is enough to desensitize anyone to even the most objectionable sights and smells, but for whatever reason I wasn't ready for what was waiting for me underneath the obese chef's cardboard portrait.

I felt my stomach drop the instant I raised the lid. Scuttling around inside the box, crawling over leftover crust, and collecting around puddles of grease like caribou at a watering hole were dozens of those little black bugs! It was by far the most I had ever seen in one place. A jolt of panic darted down my arm, causing me to drop the pest-ridden thing to the floor. The thud must have startled the insects because next thing I knew they were dispersing throughout the room, scurrying for cover in all directions.

The thunderous blare of Donald breaking wind erupted from the living room, accompanied by a beastly snort that made me cringe so hard it caused my entire body to tremble. I followed the awful noises to find my brother still sawing wood on the sofa. Sordid thoughts of Elizabeth willingly allowing that perverted snake, Chuck Volderschmidt, to defile her hallowed Garden of Eden in Jessica Brakowtzki's bathroom once again started to swirl through my mind. *It was Donald's fault.* He was the reason I had been afraid to ask Elizabeth out in the first place. All the filth he created, his disgusting lifestyle – I had been far too self-conscious to allow anyone close enough to me where they might learn the truth about him. And then it came to me – an answer so simple I was shocked I hadn't thought of it before. There was only one way that I could ever truly be happy. I had to get rid of Donald.

Before I get into the next part of my story I want to explain to you that I thought long and hard about how to deal with the situation. A crazy person might have reacted on pure impulse after coming to the realization that had just made itself plainly apparent to me. *But I'm no crazy person!* I made certain to evaluate every possible option in exhausting detail before finally deciding to kill my brother.

Once my choice had been made, I slowly crept towards the napping ogre, although I'm sure that due to the marijuana induced coma he was current-ly sleeping off, I could have been doing cartwheels and he wouldn't have woken up. Looking down at his chubby cheeks made me feel queasy. Quite hon-estly, I felt like I was about to do him a service – like putting down a mangy dog that's blind from cata-racts and suffering from arthritis. I reveled in the moment as I cautiously wrapped my hands around his flabby neck, taking care not to wake him before I was in position. Then, in one rapid movement, I threw my body on top of his, straddling his tubby torso and squeezing his throat as hard as I could. Almost immediately his eyes shot open, but his startled, terrified stare only helped to empower me. Donald may have been larger than me, but I was stronger. His muscles had atrophied due to years of lounging around the apartment while mine had become more developed from my daily outings to the gym. Desperate pleas for mercy sporadically leaked from his mouth, but I couldn't make out a word he was saying (*Nor did I care to hear them!*). I could feel his windpipe crushing under the grip of my hands. The pressure caused his eyes to bulge from his head like one of those goofy stress management toys that at least one jackass has on his desk in every single office on the planet.

It surprised me how long it took to finish the job. I must have been at it for at least ten minutes before I was sure he was dead. By the end of it, I was drenched in sweat. Lactic acid rushed through the muscles of my arms producing a mild burning sensation in my biceps and triceps. Donald's face had turned a greyish hue; black and purple rings encircled his fat neck where my hands had been choking him. His tongue hung from his mouth like a dog stuck out in the sun without a bowl of water. As I looked at my dead brother, not an ounce of remorse lingered in my consciousness. Donald had brought death on himself. As far as I was concerned, my brother was barely alive before I strangled him.

I knew that keeping him in the apartment would not be wise. Storing his corpse was something only a psychopath like Ed Gein or John Wayne Gacy would do. Eventually his body would rot and smell (*even more than the apartment itself*) and people would complain. If enough tenants raised a fuss the landlord would demand to investigate and then I'd be finished. My parent's summerhouse was only an hour and a half from the university. I was positive I could get rid of it there. All I needed to do was sneak his body to my car in the parking garage without anyone noticing.

***

Transporting Donald's corpse from the living room to my car turned out to be easier than I thought it would be. It was midterms week and most of my building's occupants were locked away inside their apartments cramming for exams or pulling all-nighters at the library.

There were always oversized cardboard boxes, discarded by tenants after whatever furniture delivered inside of them had been removed, stacked up next to the dumpster behind my building. I selected the biggest one I could find then headed back to my unit with it. Donald's limp body felt like it weighed a thousand pounds, but the adrenaline coursing through my veins gave me the strength to hoist his hefty cadaver into the box without too much difficulty. I dragged the thing down the hall, into the elevator, and up to my sedan, trying my best to appear as inconspicuous as possible. Luckily for me, I didn't run into any inquiring minds eager to know what was inside the package I was hauling. *Could you imagine!* I'd probably be forced to blubber out some sort of pitiful, Jack Tripper-esque excuse if people started asking questions. Just like an episode of Three's Company, only with less boobs and more murder!

The drive up to my parent's summerhouse was a quiet one. I didn't feel like listening to the radio and Donald wasn't in the mood to do much talking. I was surprisingly calm for having just committed fratricide. To be honest, I was more relieved Donald was dead than distraught. He was a terrible brother and from what I could tell growing up, he wasn't much of a son to my parents either. Once the matter of his body was taken care of, I would be able to get back to school and start living a normal life.

I had a plan, in case you were wondering. Only a complete whack-job would kill someone without an exit strategy. My parent's vacation home was conveniently secluded and located on a massive lake. When I was little, my father and I used to take his old rowboat out on the water before Donald or my mother would wake up so we could go fishing. We'd spend the morning together, usually catching nothing and waiting for the sun to peak out from over the eastern hills while he spouted off obscure trivia to me about the lake.

"Yup. This lake has a surface area of approximately 17 square miles." He'd say to me. "It's been measured at 518 feet at its deepest point. Better keep your arms and legs in the boat, no telling what could be down there. Just about anything could hide in a body of water this big."

He always said the last part just to get a rise out of me, but the sheer size of the lake always stuck with me. There was some truth to his teasing. *Anything could hide down there – e*ven my blob of a brother.

My plan was to dump his corpse in the lake and ditch my car ten miles south of my school (the opposite direction of my folks summer house). From there I would have to find a ride back to the campus; if I could make it to the school before people in my building started waking up, no one would realize I had even left. A little later I could report my brother missing and my car stolen. It wouldn't be hard to make it look like he had taken my car. I could leave his sweatshirt in the back seat, smear his fingerprints all over the steering wheel, and maybe even sprinkle a little of his hair around to make it seem like he was driving it. Donald had a couple minor run-ins with the law when he was younger. Nothing major – he got hit with a misdemeanor for marijuana possession when he was 17 and some vandalism stuff when he was a little younger, but compared to my squeaky clean record he looked like a felon. Convincing the police that he had finally gone off the deep end and skipped out on town wouldn't be a problem.

I pulled my car around to the back of the lake house and killed my headlights. The closest neighbors lived about a mile away, but I was taking no chances by unnecessarily drawing attention to myself. It was getting late; the clock on my dashboard flashed 11:30. The light from the numbers bathed the inside of my car in a pale green glow. For a few seconds nothing felt real to me – like I had somehow been transported into the plot of a David Lynch movie. I quickly snapped myself back to reality and got to work.

I dragged Donald's corpse out of the trunk, and lugged it down the gravel path that lead towards my father's tool shed. I had one more precaution I needed to take in order to make sure I wouldn't be caught. If watching hours upon hours of Horatio Caine catching bad guys and solving murders down on South Beach taught me anything it's that no matter how terrible the crime, there's always time for an inappropriate stomach-groaning pun (YEEAAHHHH!!!!). If it taught me anything else, it's that dental records and fingerprints are by far the easiest way to identify a body. Donald may have been dead, but he still had a mouthful of teeth and all ten of his fingers. My Dad's shed, however, stored a sturdy set of pliers and a handy pair of heavy-duty pruning sheers. I think you can put two and two together and figure out where this is going.

I rolled Donald's cumbersome corpse the final few feet through the shed's door and propped it upright against the wall. I must have inherited my affinity for tidiness from my father; he always kept his things so neat and orderly. Suffices to say, his shed was no exception. I had little trouble locating the pliers I would need to remove my brother's teeth. The operation, I estimated, would most likely be a bloody one so I decided to reel out the blue plastic tarp that was propped up in the corner in order to catch any "DNA evidence" that might escape my brother's mouth while I yanked away at his brown-ish-yellow, smoke stained incisors. I had just fin-ished laying it down on the floor when I noticed something out of the corner of my eye that made every muscle in my neck go rigid and sent a wave after wave of fright pulsating throughout my body. I blinked thrice, silently praying to God, Jesus, Bud-dha, Krishna, and any other holy deity whom might have happened to be observing the scene that what I had just witnessed out of my peripheral vision was nothing but an optical illusion. Unfortunately for me, my prayers had gone unanswered because my vision had not deceived me. Donald's chest was moving.

I was too afraid to turn my head. An hour earlier he was dead. I had even checked his pulse. *People don't just come back to life*, I told myself. That was something a crazy person would believe. Slowly, I rotated my neck in his direction in order to get a better look. What happened next was something I have not been able to forget in the days since the incident -- no mater how hard I've tried.

Donald's body still sat limp against the wall of the shed – the skin of his lifeless face had gone from grey to pale white during the drive. There was noth-ing in his cold, empty stare that would suggest any signs of vitality or even a single trace of conscious-ness, yet his chest was clearly throbbing up and down with alarming frequency. I tried to swallow, but realized my mouth had gone bone dry. With a *thud* his body slumped to the floor, causing me to jump three feet off the ground. The trunk of his core continued to **move**. He was laying on his back now; his colorless face turned in my direction. Perhaps against my better judgment, I called out to him.

"Donald?" I managed to mutter out. There was no reply. The only thing I could hear was the sound of my own heavy breathing.

Moments later, Donald's body began to stir – slowly at first, but gradually his motions became more violent. I fought back a scream as his carcass started to convulse and writhe on the shed's floor just a couple of feet from where I was standing. His arms and legs were flailing through the air while his torso shook and jerked like he was having a seizure. A low hiss seeped from his mouth – a sound that violated my ears while I trembled with fright from the scene unfolding before me.

No, this can't be happening. It can't be real, I thought to myself. But it was happening, and I can tell you with the utmost sincerity that it was very real.

The hiss grew louder. I covered my ears with my hands and shook my head in disbelief. Donald's jaw started to twitch as if he was trying to talk. I was terrified of hearing his voice – of hearing the damning words I expected to come out of his mouth. But it wasn't words that emerged from between my brother's lips that evening. *No sir!* What came out instead was much more horrifying. An endless stream of those little black bugs began to pour from his mouth, flooding the room like a biblical plague, and swarming nearly everything in sight. They scuttled along my shoes and up my pants legs. I swatted at them frantically, doing everything in my power to get the vermin off of me, but the more I brushed them away, the more they overran me. My mind was panicky; I needed to remove the filthy things from my person as soon as possible.

The lake! I remembered. Still crawling with bugs, I leapt over Donald's now motionless body, burst through the shed's door and made a break for the dock right next to my house. I was moving so fast the evening's cool air began stinging my face while I sprinted through the darkness. When I reached the end of the dock, I threw myself head first into the icy cold water without hesitation, in an attempt to drown the bugs still clinging to me.

In all the excitement and panic, I forgot to close my mouth and hold my breath before diving into the lake. The frigid water rushed down my esophagus in an effort to invade respiratory system, nearly drowning me in the freezing depths. Frantically, I kicked and thrashed underneath the surface, trying to make it to the dock's ladder while water continued to usurp the air in my lungs. With one last desperate attempt at survival, I grasped onto one of the ladder's rungs and yanked myself free from the drink, into the night air, gasping and choking in the moonlight. Exhausted, but relieved to be alive, I slogged my shaking body back up to the dock and collapsed on its deck.

I had little time to relax though; there was still work to be done. Donald's body wasn't going to dispose of itself and I knew that I needed to move fast if I wanted to be back at the school by sunrise. The bugs were mostly gone by the time I got back to the shed. They must have scattered into the back yard or the wooded area that surrounded the house when I made my dash towards the lake. A few of them had stuck around and were lingering on the floor and walls when I returned, but I could cope with that. There really wasn't time to stop and contemplate the peculiarity of what I had just witnessed. I was well aware of the inexplicable circumstances surrounding the little black bugs and Donald's body – never in my life had I ever heard or read about something so odd or terrifying, but I was on the clock. In order to secure my alibi, I needed to finish the job and get back to school.

I picked up the set of pliers, dragged my brother on top of the tarp, and kneeled down next to his corpse. Some of the insects were still trickling out of the corner of his mouth. I brushed them away and got down to business.

I pulled each and every one of my brother's teeth out with those pliers. His hands were a bit harder to remove with the shears then I thought they would be, but my father's *Dewalt Diamond Tipped Heavy Duty Hand Saw* did a satisfactory enough job. I don't know why a handsaw needs to be diamond tipped – all my father ever did with it was cut firewood, but I was more than thankful for his testosterone fueled purchase that evening. Needless to say, it sliced through my brother's wrists faster than an emo kid looking for attention.

I wrapped what was left of his body up in the blood soaked tarp and lugged it all the way back to the dock where my father's rowboat was tied up. It was late and with the weather as cold as it was, I knew I wouldn't see anyone else on the lake, not at that time of year anyways. For about twenty minutes I paddled out, not stopping until I knew I was in a place where the water would be deep. Next, I deadlifted Donald's fat carcass up from the boat and dumped it overboard. It sunk down into the murky depths, disappearing from sight like attractive people at a "Magic: The Gathering" tournament. I chucked the teeth I had extracted into the lake as well, watching them quickly scatter and vanish below the surface. When I got back to land, I used the hands I had removed to plant Donald's fingerprints all over my steering wheel and the dashboard of my car before burying them out in the woods.

I made sure to straighten up the shed so my father wouldn't find anything amiss the next time he was in it. Before I left the lake house that night, I went inside and headed up to my parent's bedroom. My father kept a revolver in the nightstand by his bed and I figured it might come in handy somewhere down the line – just a contingency plan incase things started to spiral out of control. *Crazy people don't come up with contingency plans so you can see how clear and level headed my thinking was.*

I got back in the car and fired up the engine. All I needed to do was ditch my ride; then I'd be home free. A tiny, painful *prick* on my neck startled me, momentarily breaking my concentration. I reached back and snatched the little black bug that had bitten me, pinching it between my fingers. It tried to squirm away, but I crushed it's body before it could, popping it like a pimple while I laughed maniacally at it's plight like a super villain high on shrooms.

***

I left my car in the parking lot of a Carl's Jr. about twenty minutes South East of my campus. I'm not really sure why I chose Carl's Jr. I guess it just seemed like an appropriate place for Donald's trail to run cold (one last Double Western Bacon Cheeseburger for the fat ass before his vanishing act).

The bus would be my ride back. My school was too far travel by foot so running was out of the question and I was concerned that calling a cab would be an easy way to get noticed in case the police came snooping around, looking for witnesses. I needed to stay as discreet as possible. My alibi would be a failure if someone like a cabbie, could pinpoint me in the general proximity of the car I planned on reporting stolen. Even though it was likely I would encounter people on the bus, I reasoned that since it was still early, no one would be interested in making conversation (or even eye contact) – especially not before the break of dawn.

I had studied the bus routes earlier. There was an express line I could catch that would drop me off near the school. The first bus was supposed to come by at 5:00 AM and only made a few stops before reaching the campus. I checked my watch. It was 4:30; with any luck my ride would be on time and I could make it back to the apartment before people started waking up. I took a seat on the bench and waited alone in the dark for the bus to arrive.

Just a few minutes later, a scruffy, old hobo hobbled up to the bus stop and popped a squat next to me. A pungent stench wafted through the air; I winced in the realization that I was sitting down wind from the homeless man's foul fragrance – an awful combination of urine and rancid milk. I scooted over until one of my ass cheeks was hanging off of the edge of the bench, attempting to put as much distance between myself and the terrible funk as possible. The vagrant sat hunched over with his hands inside the pockets of his dirty, ragged sweatshirt while he mumbled something incoherently to himself. His hood was pulled up over his head, covering most of his face, but from what I could see, he looked as if he was in desperate need of some dental work.

He started to rock back and forth on the bench as the unintelligible garbles spewing from his mouth became louder and more frequent. Still, I couldn't make out what the troubled man was saying. I checked my watch – it was only 4:37. I remember the time exactly because that's when things began to get strange.

We were all alone at that bus stop. Aside from the occasional car zipping by there wasn't another soul in sight. None of the stores around were open yet so there was no warm, safe place for me to duck into while I waited for the bus to show. The homeless man clenched his decaying, rotten teeth and began to violently shake his fists in the air. His ramblings had turned into a fit of angry shouting and I finally started to understand what he had been saying once the raving lunatic started barking into the dark morning sky.

"He's dead! He's dead! His own flesh and blood! His baby brother! Why!? Why, baby brother!?"

I shot up from the bench and stumbled backwards for a few steps. I told myself that he was just some maniac – that there was no way he could have known about Donald, but somewhere deep down inside me I couldn't shake the feeling that all his hooting and hollering was directed towards me. I checked my watch again; it was only 4:43. Time was moving slower than an octogenarian wearing ankle weights.

He stood up from the bench and started shambling towards me like a zombie, all the while, continuing to shout out accusations out at the top of his lungs.

"Why, baby brother!? Murder! His own flesh and blood!"

I backed off into the street, but *Nostrahomelss* followed. A flash of light illuminated the dark road we were both now standing in. I turned my head to see the bus I had been waiting for about a block away, sitting at a red light. *Salvation!* I thought to myself. It had arrived early, but before I had the chance to rejoice the mad hobo lunged at me, grasping me around my wrists with both of his hands. He lifted his head and met my terrified gaze. For the first time I could see his entire face and I felt myself get woozy from the appalling sight staring back at me.

His lips were horribly chapped – so dry and cracked that blood began to trickle from their pussy sores as he smiled his rotten grin. The bizarre homeless man's teeth were worse than I thought. The black and yellow giblets jutted out from the bum's disease ridden gums in arbitrary directions, sometimes even overlapping each other. As he continued to squawk at me, I noticed an additional sound beginning to emanate from the homeless man's mouth. It was a horrible low hiss, one that I had heard earlier that evening – in the tool shed right before the bugs began to spill from the mouth of my dead brother. I felt myself get sick at the mere thought of those things swarming me back at the lake house.

"He's Dead!" he shouted. *"Baby brother, why!? Murdered by his own flesh!"*

I was too terrified to look away. The hiss became louder as bugs began to crawl out of the homeless man's nose, scurrying down his face. I broke his grip, falling over backwards onto my rear end, and started to shuffle away on the ground as fast as I could. The light in the street got brighter and I realized the bus was advancing towards us. Seeing this, the deranged homeless man darted out of the road, leaving me sitting on the asphalt as the express line pulled up to the stop. The last thing I needed to do was miss my bus so I stood up, dusted myself off, and headed for the door.

The driver didn't even look twice at me as I boarded. I'm sure she's seen her fair share of crazy working that route. I was thankful for it too. As far as I was concerned, the less people that could pick me out of a lineup the better. There were only two other riders on the bus and both of them looked half asleep. I took a seat in the very back and tried to catch my breath.

Could he have really known about Donald?

No, I told myself. Something like that just doesn't make sense. It would be completely illogical to assume that the stinking schizoid had any knowledge of what happened between my brother and I. I was able to eventually reason that he must have been talking about someone else. *You see? A sensible person can always come up with a rational explanation for things.*

I sat in a daze for the rest of the ride back to campus, trying to erase the mental image of those bugs moving about the homeless man's face. I still see it when I close my eyes. I still hear them hissing too – only I know that's not in my head.

***

I stumbled into my apartment before daybreak. I had forgotten how messy the place was before I left. It was ok though, I took great pleasure in fixing up the place knowing it would be the last time I ever had to clean one of my brother's messes. Fatigue settled in by the time I was wrapping up and I collapsed on my bed where I fell asleep for hours. By the time I woke up, the sun was already making its descent from the sky. Every single one of my muscles ached and the joints in my arms and legs burned as if they were on fire. I realized that the night had taken a greater toll on my body than I originally anticipated. All I wanted to do was lie in bed and not move until the pain went away, but I knew my job wasn't done yet. I had to pad my alibi.

I called the police and reported my car stolen. After about an hour of waiting, an incredibly bored looking cop came by and took down my information. He seemed even less impressed when I divulged to him that my brother was the most likely culprit. The expression on the officer's face told me he'd much rather have been at the doughnut shop, sipping coffee and talking football with the rest of the boys than dealing with me. Nevertheless, I put on an act for him that even Laurence Olivier would have been jealous of.

"Oh please officer, tell me if you hear anything!? Honestly, I'm more worried about Donald than my car. I think he may have finally lost it!"

The cop nodded his head, reassured me that everything would probably be alright, and drove off in his squad car, presumably to get back to his busy day of consuming coffee and chowing down on bear claws while debating Tom Brady vs. Peyton Manning with the rest of his overweight, mustached compatriots. I was confident my performance would be enough to throw the police off my trail. Excluding the psychopath at the bus stop and the hiccup with the bugs in the tool shed, everything was going exactly as I had envisioned. It wasn't until later that evening when my plan would begin to fall apart – *and fall apart it did!* I remember the exact point things started going haywire. How could I forget? My life has become a case of situational irony akin to that of a Shakespearian comedy. And how appropriate is it that the catalyst – the very thing that got the ball rolling, was an all too familiar *prick* on the back of my neck?

***

I was sitting at the desk in my room when it happened. Disposing of my brother's body had cost me a lot of very valuable study time and I was trying to take advantage of every minute I had left before my midterm exams by burying myself in my coursework.

The sting of the insect's bite took me surprise, snapping my attention away from the textbook I was reading. I let out a yelp and twisted in my chair, attempting to swat the irritating little nuisance off of me, but paused, suddenly stricken with fear when I took notice of a sound that had begun to infiltrate the room – one I was starting to become far too acquainted with. A low hiss seeping through the walls – the hiss of those little black bugs.

The noise seemed to be loudest coming from the wall on the opposite end of my room near the foot of my bed. I approached what appeared to be its origin cautiously and ran my fingers along the wall. Terror's dark hand gripped me tight as the vibrating stucco sent tiny tremors up my fingers when I touched it. *I could feel them moving*, crawling, even squirming over top of each other, just behind the thin plaster barricade between us. The thought made the contents of my stomach rise halfway up my throat.

The hiss begun to get so loud it became deafening. I jerked my hand back from the wall as the terrible noise persisted to increase in intensity. The bedroom wall was throbbing now, just like Donald's chest in my father's tool shed one night prior. I feared that any moment the bugs would come bursting through the wall like puss spurting from the center of a ripe zit.

I barely had time to cringe in fear from the terrible sight before the hiss began to change, mutating and warping itself into something that sounded like words. The voice was inhuman – unlike anything I've ever heard before. Almost as if it was speaking to me through the sound of flesh sizzling over an open flame.

"He's dead! He's dead! Why baby brother!? Why!?"

The words pervaded my ears and burrowed themselves into my brain like a parasite. I turned to run, but toppled over the ataman, jamming my left wrist when I put my hands out in front of me to break my fall. I looked towards the wall again, where the hiss had originated; it was moving as if half of my bedroom had begun breathing.

"You killed him! Why!?"

The wall continued to swell up and down like the waves of an angry sea. I began to prepare myself for the worst. I was certain that death would be riding into my room in next to no time – a six-eyed horse-men with the mandibles of an arthropod, ready to drag my soul to hell.

"He was ours, now you'll be too! You'll be ours or we'll ruin you!"

I screamed. The wall was writhing and twisting in ways that defied physics. The entire room looked like a bad acid trip.

"You'll be ours or nothing!"

It was madness. If I didn't know for sure that my mind was so healthy and sound, I might have believed that I was losing it (Of course a crazy person would never acknowledge that kind of complete and utter insanity to be anything out of the norm. I however, was well aware of the implausible situation I had found myself in, thus proving the lucidity of my mental state of being).

I curled up into a ball and shut my eyes, cradling my head in my hands (reverting back to the most primal of self-defense mechanisms). The walls were closing in on me and the hiss had reached an unbearable pitch, but just when I thought certain doom was upon me, another noise filled the apartment – a knock on the front door.

It took me a minute for me to gather myself, but eventually I noticed that the walls had returned back to normal and that the hiss had vanished almost as soon as the knocking had begun. Another knock brought me to my feet and I proceeded to the door (albeit still shakily). To my surprise Chuck Volderschmidt and Elizabeth were standing in front of me when I opened it.

Chuck was shirtless, although his pasty white chest and sun burned forearms made him look like he was wearing a t-shirt. Elizabeth (looking as stunning as ever) was wearing nothing but an oversized G-Unit football jersey – the kind of shirt you might find bundled up on the floor at Burlington Coat Factory or Nordstrom Rack. I winced a bit once I came to the realization that it was most likely Chuck's.

"Bro," said the turd. "We thought we heard a scream! Is everything ok or were you just watching porn with the speaker turned up too loud...cause I do that some times."

"Umm, no Chuck. Thanks for your concern, but I just tripped over the ataman in my room and sprained my wrist."

"Ouch!" said Elizabeth. And it was that moment that I decided that the G in G-Unit must have stood for Goddess. "Do you need a doctor?"

I shook my head and forced a laugh, "No, no. Just startled myself. I guess I should watch where I'm going."

"Fucking-A you should," chimed Chuck. "Next time I hear a scream like that from this apartment it better be because you have a hot biatch in here! L-O-L." He actually said "LOL". Chuck grabbed a handful of Elizabeth's magnificent rump. "Come on babe. Let's get back to your apartment." He turned towards me and mouthed something that rhymes with *meeting that wussy*when she wasn't looking while thrusting his pelvis in the air and flicking his tongue between the peace sign he was making with his fingers as they walked away.

I shut the door behind me and leaned against the wall, trying to get a grasp on everything that had just occurred. Part of me was still terrified that the hiss would begin anew and my six-legged tormentors would pick up where they left off, but deep down inside, I knew they wanted me alive. The bugs were actually *speaking* to me. Not just speaking, but delivering a message – a warning.

Now you'll be ours too! You'll be ours or we'll ruin you.

I understood what they meant. Those little bastards were the only witnesses to Donald's murder. The bugs loved my older brother. He was like a benevolent god to them! They gorged themselves on the heaping piles of garbage he left lying around the apartment. The place was like a paradise for those terrible things and then I moved in and took it all away. Now they wanted me to take his place – to maintain the status quo and continue showering them with gifts. It was a threat – become as foul and nasty as my older brother, return their home to paradise or somehow they would "ruin" me.

Well, if it was a god they wanted, then it was a god they were going to get, but not the kind they were asking for. I was about to go *Old Testament* on those little black bugs.

*****

It's the police who keep knocking at my door. They won't say they're the cops. Actually, they won't say much of anything. It doesn't really matter though; I know it's them. They must be here to arrest me for what I did to Donald. I'm sure the smug sons of bitches are going to pat themselves on the back for breaking the case. *The idiots.* I was careful. They never would have known if it wasn't for those goddamned bugs.

I purchased a fogger at Home Depot the following day. I don't know much about exterminating so I let the guy at the store convince me to splurge on the most expensive one they had. It came in a canister that looked like an old Soviet warhead. On the side of it was a picture of a mushroom cloud with the words "BIG BUG BOMB" written in a bold yellow font that told me it meant business.

When I got back to the apartment, I set it up in my bedroom (the sight of my earlier run-in with the little pests). The instructions on the container said that the fogger released a cloud of poisonous gas capable of reaching a radius of 2,500 square feet, which is a distance that's easily more than twice the size of my humble living accommodations. All I had to do was pull the tab, leave the apartment for a couple hours, and let the gas do the work.

I was positive the bugs would mount an attack and come gushing through the walls in an effort to thwart me, but it never happened. I set off the bomb just like the instructions said, placed the fogger down on my desk, and escaped with zero resistance.

I thought that I'd be able to forget about everything that had taken place while I was at school that day, but unfortunately my midterm exams weren't even enough to help me ignore the constant reminders. I would look into my study materials, doing my damndest to take my mind off of the recent horrors I had experienced, but no matter how much I tried to clear my mind, terrible memories still plagued me.

At times, I could have sworn I smelled the homeless man's nauseating aroma as I ambled around the campus. I feared he would be waiting for me every time I turned a corner, shouting accusations at the top of his lungs like he had that night at the bus stop. To anyone watching, I must have looked like quite the nut, peering over my shoulder every ten feet or so, keeping an eye out for the invisible boogeyman.

Then there were the things that weren't in my head. Over the course of the day, I would catch people giving me the most judgmental, scornful looks – two girls whispering to each other and pointing in my direction as I walked by, a professor shaking his head when I turned in my test, even the barista in the coffee shop turning her nose up at me when I stopped in to get a mid afternoon pick-me-up. I was beginning to feel the paranoia seeping in. The way everyone was glaring at me, *it was as if they knew what I had done to Donald.*

I ducked into the library to get away from the judgmental sneers and disapproving stares. I needed a quiet place to think and clear my head, but the coffee I guzzled down hadn't given me the caffeine boost I was looking for and I quickly found myself nodding off at a desk in the computer lab once I settled in. My nap was far from restful though. The vividness of my nightmare saw to that.

The warmth and safety of the library faded away only to be replaced by the last place on Earth I wanted to be. I barely had time to realize I was back at the lake again, treading along the surface of the icy water I had dumped my brother in when I felt myself begin to sink. I tried to swim, but no matter how hard I kicked and paddled I couldn't free myself from the water's pull. It began to envelope me, slowly but surely swallowing my body whole. I took one last desperate gasp of air as my head submerged under the surface of the lake.

Ten feet under water and sinking fast, a sense of hopelessness began to overwhelm me. I stopped trying to fight my way to the surface.

When I reached forty feet, I could feel the pressure in my ears and behind my eyes start to build. It felt like my head was being crushed in a vice.

One hundred feet and plunging deeper, my lungs felt as though they were going to burst. No longer able to stand the pain, I opened my mouth to scream and felt the lake rush down my throat just as it had when I dove into the water the night I killed Donald.

Deeper I descended into the darkness, suffering, drowning, a victim of the water's merciless onslaught when I saw something waiting for me at the lakebed. Dread shot through my already agonizing body when I recognized what I was being pulled towards.

My brother's bloated corpse was sitting at the bottom of the lake – his body hanging halfway out of the tarp I had rolled him in. Days of water damage had turned his skin a sickening greenish white. The fish had reached him by then and a few of them were still feeding on the exposed flesh of his face as I touched down to the lake's floor. His eyeballs were gone. They're always the first to be eaten; it's the easiest part of the body for the fish to digest. I read that somewhere once. We were now face to eyeless, partially consumed face. To my horror, his puffy swollen lips began to slowly move. He was speaking to me and somehow under hundreds of feet of unforgiving, freezing cold water I could hear him.

"They're not dead," he said to me in a wheezy croaking voice. It reminded me just how hard I had squeezed his throat that night. "You can't get rid of them." He stared at me through the empty sockets of his face with the same disdain that I had once viewed him with. "They want to make you like me."

I wanted to respond, but the freezing water gagging and choking me prevented any sort of retort. A smile crossed his decaying, half-eaten face and I could tell that he was pleased by this. I'd even go as far as to say that he was laughing at my plight.

"You'll be theirs," he said. "You'll be theirs or they'll ruin you!"

A deep low hiss began to flood my ears. If the lake hadn't already collapsed my lungs I would have been shrieking at the top of them. The hiss grew louder and louder as my brother began to open his mouth. Once more the noise had become deafening. Donald's mouth had stretched far too wide (as if he had unhinged his jaw) making his horrible face even harder to look at.

Then in an instant, I was back in the library – my cheek flush against the desk I had fallen asleep on. I had woken up. It took a second for reality to settle in. I took a few hurried gasps, trying to remember what breathing felt like. The dream had felt so real. Once I got my bearings back I sat and reflected on it for a while. Donald's words had sent a chill down my spine.

They want to make you like me. He had told me. *You'll be theirs or they'll ruin you!*

I looked up. The librarian, a pretty undergrad, was scowling at me from behind her desk. Everyone I was coming in contact with seemed to hate me. There was only one possibility; *it had to be the bugs!* I found myself contemplating the plausibility of that idea. Sure it was crazy, but what other reason could there have possibly been for my recent status as a social pariah? After all, the little bastards *had* demonstrated that they had the ability to communicate. Perhaps they were talking to others, revealing to them my dirty secret. Maybe that's what they meant when they said they would ruin me.

My brother was most likely right. There was no way some stupid fogger I purchased at the hardware store was going to kill off those things. They had some sort of (I know it sounds nuts) supernatural abilities that extended way beyond resistance to insecticides. Their motives had become clear to me: either I gave into their whims, or they were going to rat me out. A feeling of desperation started to brew inside me. I needed exterminate them once and for all.

My fears were confirmed when I heard the hiss coming from my apartment before I had even made it halfway down the hall. The Big Bug Bomb had performed about as well as a quadriplegic in an Ironman competition. It didn't matter. They might have been able to fend off the noxious fumes of the fogger, but I had a new plan. If the pesticide didn't work, then maybe fire would do the trick. In my back pocket was a case of matches, in my right hand was a can full of gasoline, and in my mind was the unrelenting desire to finally rid myself of those little black bugs.

They weren't hard to find when I opened the door. The little buggers were everywhere! I locked the door behind me and quickly began splashing the walls of the living room with petrol. Again that terrible hiss started to buzz through the apartment and I knew that the bugs were assembling – preparing for war. Unlike before though, I found the sound encouraging. The bug bomb didn't even frighten them enough to warrant a reaction. The fact that they were stirring made me think that I had them on the ropes a little bit. I knew that I needed to work fast. It would be important to hit every room so the bugs wouldn't have a place to run to once I set the apartment ablaze. For once they were afraid and I was reveling in it.

"You like that you little bastards!" I shouted. "I'll teach you to snitch on me!"

After I finished in the living room I ran to the kitchen, where those awful things had first bitten me – the hiss followed close behind. Once more the appalling sound assaulting my ears began to form words.

"You can't do this! You're ours now!" I ignored their threats and continued to paint the walls and counter with gas. *"Stop this!"* the hiss commanded. I started to laugh out loud.

The bathroom was next. By the time I got in there, bugs had begun seeping out of the shower-head, trickling from the sink, even crawling their way up from the drains. I ran the faucets in an effort to drown as many of them as possible. Somehow I kept my composure long enough to spill some gasoline on the wall next to the toilet.

"STOP IT, STOP IT, STOP IT!" the nasty things screamed out at me.

I staggered out of the bathroom like a drunk girl in a nightclub and bumbled my way down the hall towards Donald's room. Even with the stench of gas spreading throughout the apartment, I could still smell my brother's distinctive funk when I entered his lair (for all I knew, it would manage to linger even after the room had been reduced to ash and embers). I had just begun dousing his bed's disgusting, bacteria riddled sheets when a sudden *thud* caught me on the back of the head, knocking me to the ground and causing me to drop the gas can. I felt my vision blur and my head become as light as a balloon – two obvious signs that I likely experienced a concussion. Blood started to dribble from back of my head where I had been struck, spilling down my neck and onto the floor – an even more obvious sign that I likely experienced a concussion.

Woozy, but still determined, I willed myself to wobbly feet. The blow to the back of my skull had raised more than a few questions in my aching head – questions that were answered as soon as my eyes began to regain their focus.

It was standing in the doorway. At first I thought it to be some sort of hallucination – an image of delirium brought on by my recent head trauma, but the longer I tried to convince myself that what I was looking at was imaginary the more I realized it wasn't. Its shape was vaguely anthropomorphic. I say vaguely because it seemed to be trying to mimic the human form, but failing miserably at it. The figure had arms, legs, and a tiny bump where the neck should be that looked like a sorry attempt for a head. It was black as soot. So dark in fact that I didn't realize at first that what I thought was its skin was actually moving. *But moving it was!* You see this lone, dark figure that had apparently struck me wasn't a single entity at all. *No sir!* It was an assemblage of those little black bugs! Millions of them all converging together like Voltron.

I scrambled for the gas can, but the abomination tackled me back down to the floor. A multitude of tiny insect legs tickled my skin as the monstrosity pinned me to the ground with its makeshift hands. It was extremely strong; I squirmed and tugged as hard as I could, but I couldn't break its grip. The hiss of the bugs was so loud at this point that I was positive my ears were going to start bleeding.

"You'll be ours! You'll be ours right now!"

The figure pinning me to the ground suddenly began to disperse as the little black bugs, thousands at a time, launched into an attack. I was swarmed with them and not just externally. They invaded every orifice of my body. I could feel them crawling up my nostrils, maneuvering in and out of my sinuses. They traveled down my trachea, using it as a tunnel, and scurried along the inside walls of my lungs. I tried to cry out, but my screams were stifled by the thousands of bugs flooding my mouth.

That wasn't the only place the nasty things decided to violate though. They entered me through every part of my body – even making themselves at home in my digestive tract and my... urethra. The pain was immeasurable. The last thing I remember was passing out in agony – that horrible hiss drowning everything out as the world faded to black.

***

I wish I could tell you that the bugs were gone when I came to or that I somehow found a way to expel them from my body, but I'm afraid that I would be lying if I did. You see, they attacked me a day ago and haven't actually stopped since.

I woke up on the floor of my brother's room in even more pain than when I had passed out. My skin is on fire from the millions of bites I've suffered since they started swarming me. The slew of bugs crawling up and down my throat makes it feel like

I'm breathing through a straw. I swallow them by the hundreds, but more just keep coming to replace them. They've probably laid their eggs inside my intestines by now.

It's ok though because I've won and they know it. That's why they called the cops on me. Even when they invaded my body, I refused to cave to their demands. I refused to become my brother and they hate me for it.

Pretty soon the little bastards won't be able to torment anyone ever again. My father's revolver is sitting in my lap as I write this and I have every intention of using i. before the police come crashing through my door. But it gets better! The carpet is still soaked in gasoline and I sure as hell don't plan on going out alone. It should only take one match to turn this whole apartment building into a scene from Backdraft.

So Adiós world – and a very special goodbye to those little black bugs. I suppose we'll meet again in Hell. I'll be smiling when I see them though...because I know the score.

***

From the *Miskatonic Times*,
October 22, 2013
6 Dead In Student Housing Fire
Police Investigating Possible Arson
Six people were killed in the tragic fire that occurred at a student-housing building located off the University campus late Tuesday night. Many of the building's tenants were able to evacuate the scene.

The building was reportedly engulfed in flames even before first responders had arrived. Witnesses say they were awoken by a gunshot coming from the apartment that the fire is believed to have started in.

"The fire spread fast," said Fire Chief Bill Marshall. "The death toll might have been much higher if the gunshot hadn't alerted many of the building's residents."

The shot is thought to have been fired by third year student, Donald Miller. Both the fire and the gunshot are suspected to have emanated from his apartment. Miller lived alone and those who had met him, described the junior to be "extremely introverted".

"I didn't know him too well," said one of his neighbors who survived the fire, "but he was always so hard on himself when we did speak. He really seemed to have self-esteem issues. It was strange, he was constantly cleaning his apartment and complaining about how dirty it was. I never saw the inside of it – I don't think anybody did, but I couldn't imagine it being as bad as he said. It seemed like every other day I would see him walking to his door with a shopping bag full of cleaning supplies."

Miller's mother and father declined to speak to the Miskatonic Times about whether or not they believed their only son was responsible for the fire, but have offered their condolences to all of those who lost loved ones in the tragic event.

Miller's body was one of the six recovered from the fire. The coroner's report states that he died from a fatal gunshot wound to the head shortly after the fire started. There were no drugs or alcohol present in his body at the time of his death. However, some of the coroner's findings have raised questions about Miller's death. According to the report, even though he was not badly burned his body was recovered with severe skin damage. These injuries do not appear to be inflicted from the fire and may possibly have been caused by insect bites. His body has been transported to St. Joseph's Medical Center so more tests can be run.

The Miskatonic Police are currently investigating Donald Miller's role in the fire.

The Eye of Ra

Jay Bennett hadn't noticed the chubby man sitting alone in the corner booth until it was nearly time to close. He had been wiping down a couple of pub tables in the bar area when he spotted him, noshing on a plate of *Big Buck's En Fuego Jalapeño Poppers* and watching Division III college football highlights play on the television mounted on the wall. There was nothing particularly interesting about the chubby patron. His brown, argyle sweater vest and khaki trousers didn't exactly command attention and his plain unassuming features did nothing to accentuate his remarkably ordinary appearance. Yet still, there was something curious about the man that Jay couldn't quite put his finger on.

Closing time meant Jay would soon be spending the next hour and a half mopping puddles of urine off the bathroom floor and hand drying dishes in the kitchen, while Trevor, his nineteen-year-old zit-faced assistant manager, played Candy Crush and browsed Facebook on his phone. Jay hated closing the restaurant – mostly because he despised answering to a lazy, community college washout almost half his age. From where he was standing, he could see Trevor sitting in the office at the back of the restaurant, staring into his phone and giggling away like an acid-dropping rave bunny at Burning Man.

Any minute, Jay thought to himself. *Any minute the little shit's gonna stroll his pimply ass out here and force me to scrub the toilets 'till they fucking shine. I just know it-*

"Um, Excuse me?" The voice that interrupted Jay's pity-party was soft and sophisticated. Right away he could sense an air of intelligence in its tone – something not commonly heard at *Big Buck's Wings & Beer*. Jay looked up to see the man in the brown argyle sweater vest waving him over to his booth. "Yes, you sir. Excuse me, but may I speak to you for a moment?"

Jay glanced back towards the office. Trevor was busy furiously tapping away at the screen of his iPhone. He let out a sigh and sauntered over to the booth.

"You need the check? We're closing soon."

"Not necessary," replied the chubby fellow. "I already cleared my tab with the pretty young thing who works behind the bar."

Jay tossed the towel he was holding over his shoulder and folded his arms across his chest like a nightclub doorman. "Then what can I do for you, mister?"

"Well," the man paused briefly to collect his words. "You're Jay Bennett, correct?"

Hearing his name come out the mouth of a total stranger felt like an unexpected punch to the gut.

"I am," Jay said, doing his best to appear unmoved by the chubby man's inquiry. It was defense mechanism he had developed during his stint in prison. Jay found out very fast while serving his time that the best reaction to an unforeseen predicament was typically having no reaction at all. "And you are?"

"Oh yes, where are my manners?" The man in the sweater vest extended a sweaty palm out towards Jay. "My name is Robert Wilkins. Uh, Doctor Robert Wilkins." Jay remained silent, stonewalling the doctor, causing him to retract his hand. The chubby man studied the ex-con silently before continuing on. "FYI, I'm not the kind of doctor who went to med school. My degrees are cultural anthropology and archeology – Ancient Egyptian studies to be exact. My colleague and I have published hundreds of papers on the subject. Feel free to look me up if you don't believe me. A quick Google search should confirm my claims."

"Honestly, I don't really give a shit," grunted Jay. "What is it that you want, already?"

The doctor neatly folded his napkin and used it to dab his brow – a mannerism reminiscent of a 19th century plantation owner. "Right. I suppose there's no further need for introductions. Might as well get right down to it. Jay Bennett, I'm here tonight because I have a job for you."

"I already have a job. And if you're trying to hire me to do something illegal, then look elsewhere. I'm on parole and I don't plan on going back to prison any time soon."

Jay snatched the towel from his shoulder and started towards the bathrooms.

"Wait! Please!" the doctor desperately blurted out. "This job pays well I promise!" Jay spun around with every intent to tell him off, but froze when he spotted the sly smile that had crawled its way across the chubby man's face. " Besides, it's a hell of a lot more fun than scrubbing toilets."

***

The doctor waved a hand, inviting Jay to sit across the table from him. With two pudgy fingers he nudged his plate of Jalapeño poppers aside then bent over to retrieve a black leather briefcase that had been sitting at his feet. Jay scooted in to the other side of the booth. He swiveled his head to glance back at the office. Trevor was still gawking like an idiot into his phone.

"How do you know my name?" Jay asked.

"My associate gave me your information," he said. "Who you are. What you do. Where to find you. He told me about your criminal record. Twelve counts of burglary, three counts of drug trafficking, and assault with a deadly weapon. He said you beat a man with a crowbar?"

"I was defending myself. The guy shot my partner."

"Yeah, after the two of you broke into the man's house. You're lucky he made a full recovery or else you'd probably still be locked up. I'm surprised you even found a gig at a hole like this."

Jay glared at the doctor, his lips twisted into a frustrated scowl.

"I'm not here to judge though. After all-" the chubby man popped the latches of his briefcase and lifted the lid, "I was hoping to encourage you to break the law one more time."

He removed a red envelope from his briefcase and placed it on the table, pinning it with his index finger. "What do you know about Egyptian mythology, Jay?"

"I know a little."

"Have you ever heard of Ra, the sun god?"

"I think so," answered Jay. "He's the one with the bird head, right?"

"Very good!" a proud light beamed in the doctor's eyes. "That is correct. Ra is the *most* important god in Egyptian mythology. He was believed to have ruled over the sky and earth. And his head wasn't just that of any bird. Most often, it was depicted as either a falcon or hawk. Now, this was no accident. You see, birds of prey have the keenest of eyesight and legend has it, the Eye of Ra could see all."

He scooted the envelope across the table towards Jay then lifted his finger, releasing it before renewing his spiel.

"There's three thousand dollars cash, a photograph, an address, and a phone number in that envelope, Jay. The money is yours whether you take the job or not. If you do accept my offer, there will be an additional $7,000 in it for you. The photograph is of an artifact I'm asking you to steal for me. It's called the Eye of Ra. It's a very rare gold coin with an extremely special engraving in it. It was excavated during a dig I helped oversee one year ago and I want it back."

"And the address is where I can find it?" Jay was already thumbing through the envelope's contents.

"Yes. It's the home of an ex-colleague of mine. He's the one who has taken it. It shouldn't be too difficult for a man like yourself to retrieve. He doesn't own a gun and I'm certain he never turns on his home security system. Plus he's blind. I mean, all you have to do is keep your mouth shut and there's no way he could ever identify you. Call the phone number once you have the Eye of Ra in your possession. We will arrange a rendezvous point and I will gladly pay you the rest of the money when you hand it over to me."

"This artifact is worth a lot of money?" asked Jay.

The doctor laughed. "No monetary value other than the gold it's made from, which by the way, wouldn't get you as much as I'm willing to pay. However, for me the artifact is priceless."

The doctor snapped his briefcase shut, quickly securing the latches before standing up from the table.

"Hold up, where are you going?" asked Jay. "I still a lot of questions. Why me?"

"Every single one of your questions will be answered soon, Jay, but I'm afraid I don't have time to stick around right now. You're a skilled thief. This job will be a cinch for you. Call me tonight when you have the Eye of Ra."

"Tonight?"

The chubby man in the brown argyle sweater vest flashed him a haughty smile.

"Goodnight, Jay. Hope to hear from you soon."

Jay tucked the envelope into the waistband of his pants as he watched the peculiar patron amble out the door. A shrill high-pitched screech suddenly broke the silence of the now empty restaurant floor.

"Bennett!" Jay twisted around in his chair to see Trevor's lanky frame hovering in the office doorway. "Big Buck doesn't pay you to sit on your ass! Get in the bathroom before I call your P.O! I want to be able to eat off those toilets!"

***

The rest of Jay's shift seemed to fly by as he mulled over the doctor's proposition. Every now and then he'd run his fingers across his waist, feeling for the contours of the envelope still stuffed inside his pants, just to make sure he hadn't dreamed the whole conversation up. The doctor had told him the gig paid $10,000 – more money than he made in three months wiping down tables and washing dishes. He thought about how degrading it was working under Trevor. There was only four months left on his parole and he had already decided he was going to quit his humiliating court appointed job as soon as he was out from under the thumb of the justice system.

That kind of cash would really help out until I could find a new way to make some money, he thought to himself while puffing on his after work cigarette in the parking lot of *Big Buck's.*

Jay tugged the envelope from his jeans and searched through it until he found the photo of the artifact. An icy cold chill swept through him as he gazed down to the picture in his hand. The design etched into the face of the coin was breathtaking – a pattern so mesmerizing Jay didn't even notice the cigarette fall from his mouth while he ogled it. All at once, he felt the urge to hold the coin – to grip it between his fingers.

"The Eye of Ra," Jay whispered.

His decision had been made. Not more than a minute later he was punching the address into his GPS as he pulled his car out of the parking lot.

***

The clock on Jay's dashboard flashed 2:00AM by the time he pulled up to the house his navigation system had directed him to. He killed the engine and stared out the window at his target for what felt like an eternity, watching for signs of life. With any luck, the doctor's former colleague was out of town and Jay would be able to search the residence at his leisure. He slipped his hand into his sweatshirt pocket and gripped the handle of his butterfly knife – a safeguard he hoped he wouldn't need to use.

Jay exited his vehicle and crept around the back searching for an open window. The home was in a fairly secluded area with no visible nearby houses, virtually eliminating the possibility of nosy neighbors and unexpected eyewitnesses. It was the kind of place that a cat burglar dreamed of hitting.

Jay slinked his way through the shadowy yard towards a wide arched window in the back of the house. With a gentle nudge of his hand against the glass it swung open, allowing him to slip inside.

The doc just might have been right about this being an easy job, Jay thought. *This guy doesn't even lock his windows.*

He was now standing in a living room decorated with expensive looking furniture and ostentatious art. Hanging on the wall was a replica of Picasso's *The Weeping Woman.* Jay examined it closely, trying to discern if it had any value, even going so far as to lift it from its hanger, before he noticed the Aaron Brother's Art Mart sticker tag that was still attached to the back of the frame.

"No need to hang it back up, Mr. Bennett, I never liked that piece anyways. My ex-wife decorated the place."

The voice stopped Jay dead in his tracks.

"Yes, Mr. Bennett. I know you're down there. Won't you please join me in my study?"

Jay leaned the painting against the wall, and scanned the room searching for the source of the voice.

"The study, Mr. Bennett! I'm in my study upstairs."

He located the staircase in the foyer. Without a word, Jay removed the knife from his pocket and tiptoed up the steps. The voice had identified him by name. Panic shot through every inch of his body. Visions of once again donning an orange jumpsuit began swimming through his mind like deformed, mutant goldfish in the New York City sewers.

"Second door on the right," the voice called out when he reached the top of the stairs.

The floorboards squealed under Jay's feet as stepped down the dark hallway towards the door the voice appeared to be emanating from. He paused when he reached it and squeezed the handle of his knife tight in his fist. There was no hint of light leaking out from underneath the door. Whoever was waiting for him in the room was doing so in pitch-blackness.

"No need to knock, Mr. Bennett." answered the voice. "I'm already expecting you."

Jay pushed down on the handle and cracked the door. Its hinges seemed to scream as he opened it just wide enough to poke his head through. There was no visibility. With his free hand he yanked his cellphone free from his back pocket, turned on the screen, and waved it in front of him, bathing the room in a pale blue light.

Floor to ceiling bookshelves lined both sides of what looked to be an office. At the wall directly opposite Jay was an elegant cherry wood desk. Sitting behind it in a leather office chair was an elderly bearded man. Jay cringed when he looked closer to see the upper half of the man's face completely wrapped in bandages.

He turned his head in Jay's direction. "Come on in, Mr. Bennett. I promise I don't bite."

Jay pushed the door all the way open and took a couple timid steps inside the room.

"I hear you're looking for the Eye of Ra," said the old man – a perverse smile warped his wrinkled face. "Well, it must be your lucky day because you've come to the right place."

"I don't want to hurt you," warned Jay, "but I'm prepared to. Just give me the coin and I'll be on my way."

The old man scoffed.

"Ha! You don't want to hurt me?! Unfortunately that's not for you to decide!"

"Listen-"

"Quiet, Mr. Bennett!" the old man snapped. "You'll be leaving with the Eye of Ra tonight. There's no question in that, but I figured I'd at least disclose to you a little about the Hell you're about to unleash on yourself first. My associate, Dr. Wilkins, already told you about the coin. We excavated it a year ago during a dig of an ancient unmarked tomb recently discovered 53 kilometers outside of Cairo."

"Dr. Wilkins?" asked Jay.

"Yes, Dr. Robert Wilkins, my associate – the man who hired you to steal the artifact. Who do you think requested him to seek you out? I'm afraid you've been set up, friend. I know that must come as a bit of a shock."

"I'm not shocked," replied Jay. "I just don't believe you."

The old man smirked.

"Oh you will in time. Now, where was I? Ah yes, the dig. Wilkins and I were able to recover quite a bit from the tomb – most of which is currently touring the country, travelling from museum to museum. The exhibit is quite lovely and I'd advise you to give it a visit next time it stops back in town, but that won't be necessary."

Jay darted towards the old man and swung his knife downwards, burying it in the desk's polished wooden face.

"That's enough! Just give me the coin or the next time I stick this knife in anything it's going to be your neck!"

The old man opened the drawer of his desk and extracted a small leather pouch from it. Now that he was closer, Jay could make out brown splotches speckling the bandages that covered his eyes – dry crusty blood. It looked like the wraps hadn't been changed in ages.

"The coin is right here, Mr. Bennett, but I hope you don't think you've intimidated me into giving it to you. It will be yours in time, but I will finish telling you my story first."

"Listen I don't care about-"

"Not all of what we recovered from the tomb made it to the exhibit though," the old man continued. "You see, the coin in this bag conveniently went missing without anyone else even knowing it existed. I discovered it myself, in the hand of one of one of the mummified corpses we found in the tomb – a young priestess no older than sixteen when she was buried. It goes against my code of ethics to take *souvenirs* from an excavation, but the coin...well just look for yourself."

He reached his fingers into the pouch drew out a gold coin about the same size as a fifty cent piece then placed it on the desk in front of him. Jay held his breath. The design etched into its face was hypnotic – far more captivating in person than it was in the photo.

"The Eye of Ra," the old man whispered.

Jay reached out an arm, but the old man snatched it up before he could grab it.

"Not yet!" he shouted. "I'm not done with my story! I discovered something fascinating about this artifact very soon after taking it in my hand. It passed on to me a strange ability – a sort of clairvoyance if you will. I could sense things, Mr. Bennett. I knew what others were thinking before they said it – what things would happen before they actually occurred. Soon after, these powers took on other attributes. I learned I could read minds, anyone's I wanted. I didn't' even need to be in the same room as them – hell the same continent even! That's how I discovered my wife was having an affair."

Jay tried to say something, but he couldn't find the words. His eyes remained glued to the coin in the old man's hands.

"Dr. Wilkins was the only other person I ever shared this secret with, but even he doesn't understand what my powers would eventually become. He thinks they just drove me mad, but he doesn't understand. He doesn't understand that the Eye of Ra really does see all!"

"Give me the coin," muttered Jay. "I...I need it."

The old man laughed.

"Of course you do! I knew that the power was getting to be too much once I realized I couldn't turn it off. The thoughts of billions of people all streaming through my mind was maddening in its own right, but that was just the tip of the iceberg really. The Eye of Ra's true power is much more horrifying. Imagine, Mr. Bennett. Imagine being able to see everything! Everything that ever did exist and everything that ever will exist! My eyes no longer perceived the world the way that you do. My mind no longer experienced time in a linear fashion. I've seen it all; all the good, and yes, Mr. Bennett, all the evil as well. I witnessed Vikings rape and pillage civilizations that no longer exist. I viewed countless genocides occur throughout the course of human history. I looked through the terrified eyes of a 12-year-old Pakistani girl in the year 2087, as the heat of a nuclear bomb engulfed her and her schoolmates in flames.

The old man whipped his hand up to his face and began tearing away at his bandages.

"I couldn't take it anymore, Mr. Bennett! I couldn't bear to look any longer! That's why I did something about it! That's why I dug my eyes out of my face!"

Jay recoiled at the horrid sight now in front of him. Two gaping blood caked craters sat in place of eyes on the man's mutilated face.

"Dr. Wilkins believed he was helping me con you into transferring the curse, but he doesn't realize it doesn't work like that. It won't transfer; it will spread. Even removing my eyes has only given me temporary relief. The visions are already starting to come back to me. Soon, they'll dominate my every thought again. The only way to be rid of it is to die."

"You're fucking insane!" shouted Jay.

"And you're in denial. There's no point trying to convince you anyways. You'll learn the truth soon enough. You're the next man to bear the burden of this power. I've already seen it. That's why I had Wilkins convince you to come here. There is no escaping time, Mr. Bennett. Tonight you will wield the Power of Ra just as I have and I...tonight I will die and finally be free of this wretched curse!"

The old man stretched an arm out and ripped Jay's knife from the desk. Without warning, the maniac dove at him, slicing the blade wildly through the air. Jay grabbed hold of his arm knocking the blade away, but dropped his cellphone as they wrestled to the ground. With Jay's only source of light gone, darkness once again enveloped the study. The old man was stronger than he had anticipated. Jay gagged as the blind lunatic wrapped a hand around his throat. It felt as though he was crushing his trachea. Jay reached his arm out, desperately searching in the blackness for something to strike his attacker with. A hard plastic object brushed up against his fingertips and instantly he knew what it was. Jay wrapped his hand around the handle of his knife then thrust his it upwards until he felt it penetrate flesh.

The grip began to loosen around Jay's neck and with a thud the old man slumped to floor. Jay could feel the warmth of his blood begin to pool around both of their bodies. He pawed around on the ground for his cellphone, eventually finding it underneath the cherry wood desk. A pale blue light swam back into the room when he powered the screen back on.

The old man's body lay motionless on the floor, the point of Jay's butterfly knife submerged deep within the side of throat. Jay leaned against the desk and gasped for air. Under the light from his cellphone the blood still spilling from the old man's neck took on a deep purple hue. Jay bent over, yanked the blade from his throat then wiped it down on a part of the carpet the old man hadn't gushed on.

In the dead man's hand Jay spotted the coin. He pried the artifact from the corpse's fingers and stumbled out the door. An ice-cold shiver ran up his spine, causing his body to tremble when he looked down to the bewitching artifact resting his palm. There was something strangely comforting about holding it.

When he made it outside to his car, Jay searched through the red envelope the doctor had given him until he located the phone number then dialed it into his keypad.

"I'm sorry, but the number you're trying to reach has been disconnected. Please hang up and try again."

Jay cursed into his phone at the automated message. He had been given a fake number. He sighed and started up the engine of his car. At least he still had the doctor's name. It wouldn't be hard to look him up. Now that Jay had a homicide on his hands, he figured he'd pay the doctor a visit in order to tie up any loose ends. As Jay pulled away from the house he reflected on what the crazy old man had said to him.

The Eye of Ra see's all. What a crock of shit. He thought.

A pair of headlights approached in the distance from the opposite direction. Ever so briefly, Jay felt his brain go numb as a static image appeared in his head – a picture he could see in his mind's eye.

"It's a blue Dodge Neon," he unconsciously blurted out.

A 2005 marine blue Dodge Neon drove past his car.

The Woman In The Red Sundress

The wind feels amazing as it whips past my face. There she is. She is but a speck in the distance, but she's there, the woman in the red sundress. She doesn't know me, but I will meet her very soon. This I promise.

I wonder when we meet what she'll sound like, what she'll smell like, what she'll feel like. I wish I could freeze this moment in time just so I could admire her from afar, but alas, the woman in the red sundress grows closer.

You can never truly appreciate the majesty of the city unless you've seen it like I'm seeing it right now. It's breathtaking. The chaos and disorder of this metropolis – rough and rowdy city streets I've traveled so many times. They seem to transform into a picture of serenity and tranquility from here. *Still, the woman in the red sundress grows closer.*

Her hair is raven colored with auburn streaks. I can see it more clearly now. I close my eyes and stretch my arms like a bird, letting my other senses do the work. The freedom overwhelming my body is intoxicating. It's as if all my sorrows and all my anxiety have escaped me. And though my eyes are shut tight, I know the woman in the red sundress grows closer.

After a few moments I open my eyes again. People are looking at me now. A balding man in a suit with a briefcase points up at me.

"Look out!" he shouts.

I don't care. I feel incredible, like a shooting star that's journey is finally coming to an end after eons of aimlessly wandering the cosmos. I can see her face now. The woman in the red sundress is staring at me. She's so beautiful. Her candy red lipstick matches her ensemble. I can even smell her perfume. Its lavender scented. I had guessed it would have been citrusy, but I am not disappointed. She reaches her hands to the sky as if she's beckoning me. I can almost touch her now. She screams-

Splat

POW

As far as I know the mission is still classified and I'm pretty sure that I could get into a whole lot of trouble for recounting the events of that night. Hell, I've heard about guys getting court-martialed for less. Back when I was doing basic, I heard about a story out in San Diego, about about a Naval Officer who was rung up for sticking his dick in a subordinate's glass of chocolate milk. *Chocolate milk.* I mean, I love a tall glass of milk as much as the next guy, but is that really a reason to strip a man of his accomplishments? *Of his dignity?* Someone who's devoted his whole life to defending the rights and freedoms of his country? If you ask the Navy it was. God help the serviceman who does anything to rock the boat. Well, I have a feeling that this little story of mine is going to do a whole hell of a lot of boat rocking.

Thing is, I'm not in the U.S. Military anymore so I don't really give a damn what Uncle Sam thinks. Besides, it seems like now days any ex *trigger puller* who's seen his fair share of shit is cashing in on a book deal or getting some pretend tough guy, Hollywood actor to play them in a movie. The difference between them and me is that I'm not doing this for the money or fame. I'm doing it because I feel like I have to – *like I have an ethical obligation to keep the public informed.* Part of me hopes that others will read this story and remember what my unit and I went through. If so, then maybe they'll be able to recognize the signs that I wasn't able to see. Maybe they'll be able to trust their gut enough to ask the right questions when things just don't add up. The other part of me thinks that I've gone completely insane for even entertaining the idea that inspired me to write this.

Before I go too far, please understand that if you're expecting this to be some sort of moralistic tale about the horrors of war or a political statement about the United States' foreign policy, think again. I never was much for politics and as far as I'm concerned, anyone who's gotten paid to kill (be it for country or otherwise) doesn't really deserve a seat at the table when discussing what's right and what's wrong with this world.

Once my story is out, there won't be any hiding where it came from. If the CIA wants to find me and lock my ass up in Gitmo, it shouldn't be too hard so I might as well lay all my cards out on the table. My name is, James Williar. From 1996 to 2008 I was an active member of the military. For seven of those years I served as team leader for an Elite Special Forces unit for the U.S. Green Berets. As a member of the United States Army Special Forces I've pretty much done it all – from providing protection to foreign diplomats in war torn countries to assisting in the raid of South American drug compounds. It was the type of job that takes you all over the world. Before I turned 28, I had been to four different continents and visited over two dozen countries.

This particular story takes place in February of 2002, when my unit was called upon to take out what we were told was a suspected terrorist training complex nestled within Afghanistan's Hindu Kush Mountains.

It was a different time. America had just invaded Afghanistan; most of the world was still reeling from September 11th. The war's approval rating was through the roof and the whole damn country was out for blood. My unit was no different. We were hungry, we wanted in on the action. It was personal for us soldiers back then. Maybe that's why we were so eager to jump into a fight even though we knew there was something unusual about the job we had been selected for.

Even in briefing, the details surrounding the mission didn't smell right. A lot of us knew it too, but like I said before, we didn't care. Besides, I learned a long time ago that you don't get anywhere in The Army by asking questions. When your superiors order you to do something, you do it. What you don't do is poke and prod for additional information. They'll give you all the intel you need to know to get the job done, but not an ounce more. Compartmentalizing is what they call it. That's how the higher ups like to operate things. Everyone's just a cog in the machine, working together to serve a higher purpose.

We were told that the compound was located on the outskirts of a small isolated village about

150 Klicks due east of the Afghanistan-Pakistan border. Only about one hundred people, mostly impoverished villagers, lived in the area surrounding the training center. Twice a month, a group of Islamic extremists, believed to be associated with the Haquanni Network, would drive a truckload full of food and rations to the locals and distribute it out. This was considered strange behavior because the villagers didn't appear to produce anything useful of note.

Often times, terrorist organizations offer assistance to groups of people who harvest and cultivate marijuana or poppies (used for opium). For just the price of a few goats, some bread, and cheap medical supplies, they can turn around and sell the crops for big money to help fund their outfit. However, in the case of this particular village, the people were never asked give a thing – and still the insurgents would show up with supplies. Just to be clear, these weren't benevolent militant radicals. They were known to be ruthless drug smugglers and arms dealers – psychopaths hiding under the guise of religious revolutionaries. Intel had more than enough evidence linking them to some pretty horrific stuff, including the rape and pillage of a small village that was being extorted by a rival group. Thirty-two men and boys executed while the women – even the young girls – were sold to sex traffickers in Eastern Europe. To these people, human life held little value. They didn't just do things out of the goodness of their hearts.

Even more peculiar than the relationship between the terrorist group and the villagers was the facility that we had been instructed to hit. It had been known about for some time, but satellite images suggested that it hadn't even been active since July of 2001, a few months before the 9/11 attacks. All indications pointed to the place being completely deserted, yet we had been passed the incongruous orders to infiltrate and terminate any and all terrorist threats residing inside the compound. Keep in mind, a drone strike could do the exact same thing – quicker and more efficiently too, but for some reason Washington decided to send us.

All of this left us a little baffled as to why exactly *our* number had been called. Even though we weren't used to getting the whole story, it seemed like we had been afforded even less information than usual. It was obvious to most of us that something was definitely up. A few of the boys even joked after the briefing that all the *hush hush* surrounding the assignment might have meant that they were sending us in after Osama. Of course if we really were being sent to scratch a big name off Uncle Sam's hit list, we probably would have been informed to keep an eye out for him. That's usually the protocol with high profile targets – information even a cog could find use for.

Two black hawk helicopters airlifted twelve of us in the same night we were briefed. The choppers touched down right in front of the facility just long enough for us to put our boots to the ground before taking off again into the night sky. They weren't going far though; I was told that they'd be available for air support if things got too heavy for us on the ground.

Aside from the buzz of the helicopters fading off over the mountaintops, there wasn't a sound in the air that evening. We may have been flown in under the cover of night, but if someone really was in the compound, then it would have been impossible not to hear us coming from miles away. In the village, a few curious locals began stepping out of their huts to see what all of the ruckus was about. As the team leader, I told my men to think of them as civvies and not to engage unless given orders to fire.

I remember how uncharacteristically warm the weather was for February in Afghanistan. The heat and humidity felt artificial as we stood underneath the stars that night – as if it was being syphoned in from another climate. I could feel the perspiration begin to collect on my forehead as the abnormally muggy desert air swathed my unit. It was smothering.

The compound wasn't massive, but right away I could tell it would take a while to do a proper sweep. From the drop off point the main building looked to be somewhere around 4500 square feet, although it felt like a palace, towering over the tiny, flimsy huts of the villagers. A ten-foot cement wall ran all the way around the perimeter of the large grey building, fortifying the facility and giving it the look of a penitentiary. Thinking back, I find it kind of amazing that they were able to get the materials they needed to erect the impressive structure all the way up into the mountains considering there was only one windy dirt road that accessed the area.

We proceeded with caution to the south end of the facility where we found the gate chained shut and secured with a single padlock. The odd thing was, it was facing outwards towards us as if whoever locked it did so from the outside. One quick snip from a pair of bolt cutters later and we were through the gate, standing in the courtyard of the compound.

We found no surprises behind the walls. It was laid out exactly how the photos had suggested in the briefing. There was a couple of latrines and an empty, unlocked storage shed, but aside from that, little else. The building itself had no windows, making it impossible to get a glimpse of anyone who might have been waiting for us inside.

I broke my unit up into three teams of four – each one lead by a different soldier fluent in Farsi, the main language spoken in Afghanistan. Sergeant Horrowitz, my unit's Warrant Officer, was the most fluent so I left him in command of the team at the entrance of the compound. The villagers appeared to be getting more curious so I instructed Horrowitz to warn them off if they got too close. The other two teams, one lead by Sergeant Nichols, who was also fairly proficient in the regional dialect, and the other lead by myself, were tasked with breeching the facility using the doors located on the Eastern and Western ends of the building. Once inside, our mission was to clear the compound and make sure no potential terrorist threats were left alive. All three teams were to remain in radio contact at all times.

Before we entered the facility, I made sure my entire team was alert and on their toes. Even though satellite images hadn't spotted anyone on the premises in eight months, I wasn't about to let my unit get caught with our pants around our ankles.

There's really no way to describe the kind of adrenaline rush you feel when you know that at any point, the place could erupt into a firefight. It's that sense of walking into the unknown – the idea that death could be waiting for you just around the corner that gets your blood pumping like nothing else. It's some sort of sick combination of excitement and fear. You could liken it to the sensation you get right before your rollercoaster hits its first drop, only multiplied by a thousand.

There was no firefight though. No gunshots, no militant extremists, *no nothing* waiting for us on the first floor. The place was just as empty and uninhabited as our intel had suggested. No, not empty, that's not the right word. It was *abandoned*. As if whoever was there got up in the middle of whatever they were doing and left. Loaded guns were propped up against the wall, half-eaten moldy bowls of crud were sitting on the tables, there were even prayer mats laid out across the floor. From the looks of it, the place had been deserted for a long, long time.

We rendezvoused with Nichols and his team after a quick sweep. I ordered them to look for any hidden doors or exits while my team headed upstairs to the building's second level. We had just started our ascent up the steps when I heard Horrowitz – still out by the gate – chime in on my headset.

"Captain Williar, the civvies are grow'n in numbers, sir. We got 'bout three dozen of 'em out here right now."

"How close are they," I asked.

"Still 'bout a hundred meters away."

"Sit tight," I said. "Try not to get spooked. It's not every day a couple o' choppers land in your back yard. They're probably wondering what the hell is going on. If they get closer, warn them back. Do not use force unless it is absolutely necessary."

"Copy that."

Click.

I could definitely tell Horrowitz was jumpy over the com. I don't blame him, I probably wouldn't be all that comfortable either if I was tasked with staving off a growing mob of restless villagers. He and the rest of his team were outnumbered 9:1 out there. Still, for whatever reason, I'd have gladly switched places with him. There was something rotten in the air and it wasn't the developing situation outside that was tripping my alarm.

Expertly trained marksmen carrying high tech weaponry flanked me as we started to sweep the second floor of the compound, but still I felt small. My nerves were working overtime. It had gotten hard for me to breath, like a thousand pound weight was sitting on my chest. I had become aware of an appalling sense of dread pervading its way through my consciousness. Each room we entered seemed to have a sort of unnerving consistency to it – discarded Korans lying on the floor, half-drunk canteens of water, stockpiles of fully automatic weapons left unattended. It was as if everyone had simply gone *poof* and disappeared.

I couldn't shake the feeling that at any moment we would be stumbling upon something too horrifying for words. It wasn't terrorists I was worried about. I think subconsciously, I felt like something much worse than armed insurgents was waiting for us in the upstairs rooms.

"Willi, this is Nichols." *Willi* was Sergeant Nichol's nickname for me. He knew I found it annoying, but insisted on calling me that, especially during missions where correcting him wasn't high on my priority list. "We found a door down here on the south-east end of the complex. Looks like it leads to a basement. Could be a tunnel down there. We're going to check it out."

"Ok, let us know if you find something," I replied.

"Will do."

Click.

We only had a couple more rooms to clear and our sweep of the upstairs would be done, but I was still on edge. The ominous sense of dread that I had been feeling was growing stronger with each and every passing minute. A terrible notion floated through my mind; like we were being funneled down a deep dark hole, into the expecting jowls of some sort of carnivorous hellion with a ravenous appetite waiting for its next meal.

I've been on hundreds of missions and never felt as hopeless as I did advancing through that dark corridor towards that final room. It was different from the others; I could feel it – almost as if it had been the source of the dark aura that I had recognized the moment we stepped foot in the facility. Its door was noticeably bigger, easily twice the size of the ones in the rooms we had cleared. I practically swallowed my tongue when I noticed the strange symbols and hieroglyphics carved into the paneling. I may not be able to *read* Farsi, but I know the language when I see it written. Like I said, my job has taken me all over the world. I've been immersed in dozens of different cultures, but those markings were unlike anything I've ever seen before – completely alien in nature. I reached for the handle, but stopped short when I heard Horrowitz's voice crackle over the com system again.

"Sergeant Williar, we have a situation. The villagers are armed. I repeat, the villagers are armed."

"What? What do you mean? How many of them are armed?"

"All of 'em, sir. They're waiving their guns around and hollern'. Would you like us to engage?"

"Negative! Do not fire on those villagers. You have cover behind the walls, but the four of you don't have enough fire power to pick a fight with thirty armed and angry Afghans." I tried to radio Nichols and his team in order to send them out to the gate for support, but they weren't responding. I assumed they had lost the signal when they went underground.

Horrowitz spoke up again. "Sir, there's twice as many of 'em now. I'd say closer to sixty."

"And they're all armed?"

"Affirmative, I don't know how they got their hands on a stockpile like this, but if I had to guess I'd say every able-bodied man and boy in the village is out here right now. Thing is – and I know this sounds nuts – but they don't seem aggressive."

"What do you mean they don't seem aggressive?" I asked.

"Well, it looks like they're trying to wave us over to 'em. Some of 'em got their hands in the air and not a single one is point'n their weapons directly at us. They keep yelln' stuff, but it don't sound like threats."

"Can you hear what they're saying, Horrowitz?"

"Yeah," he said, "but it don't make much sense, sir."

"Well, what *are* they saying?!" I demanded. I was biting my bottom lip, praying our chances of getting out of that place didn't come down to a gunfight between us and sixty pissed off Afghan villagers.

"They're...they're saying to get away from the building. That the weapon will kill us."

"What!? Are we dealing with an IED here? Is this place booby-trapped!?"

"No, I don't think so...I mean, I don't know. It's hard to tell cause there's so many holler'n and they're so far away. They say we need to leave and lock the gate...that we can't trust *you* anymore. They're sayn' that the buildn' – it's damned and y'all are too."

It sounded like the kind of ridiculous heretic you always hear in that part of the world. *The building is damned.* They might as well have been telling us that *our souls were destined to rot in hell* or that *Allah was about to smite us,* but there was something about the compound that was making me feel anxious and the villagers "warnings" weren't helping to ease those sentiments. We only had one more room to clear and then I could figure out how to deal with the situation outside, but working up the will to finish our sweep was getting increasingly difficult. I was actually looking forward to getting out there and facing off with the gun-toting villagers. That's how bad I wanted to leave that god-awful place.

"Alright, sit tight," I instructed Horrowitz. "We'll be out there as soon as we finish in here."

"Roger, just be careful, sir."

Click.

I looked back to the large door with strange markings carved into it. I can't speak for the rest of my team, but the sight of it sickened me. I pushed through my sudden irrational feelings of disgust and tried the handle. It was locked of course. A couple of us put our shoulders to the door, but it we couldn't get it to budge. The thing was solid as a rock. I racked my brain, trying to figure out the best way to breach it. There was no way to predict what was behind the door. We had already found weapons in the complex and if the room contained any sort of flammable materials then a controlled explosion would be dangerous.

The sound of Nichol's voice over the com interrupted my train of thought.

"Willi, I'm here at the base of the stairs on ground level. I think we lost radio contact when we were down in the basement."

"Then you didn't hear Horrowitz," I replied. "Looks like the situation outside is getting worse. Those villagers may not be friendlies."

"I didn't hear gunshots. How bad is it?" he asked.

"Stable for now, but barely. I don't know how much longer we have until things get serious. You need to get your team out there while I finish up here."

"Copy that, but we can't leave until I show you what we found in the basement." That was the last thing I needed to hear. If I spent any more time in that building, I felt like I was going to lose my mind.

"I think," he continued, " that we might have found out what happened to some of the terrorists we were sent here to take out. I got six corpses down here and one warm body."

There were two things that had made themselves immediately present to me. First and foremost, Horrowitz and the others were sitting ducks out there without any backup or support and we needed to get back to them as soon as possible. Secondly, as bad as I wanted to get out of that building, I couldn't in good conscience leave until we had combed every last square inch of the place – and that meant checking out what Nichols was talking about. I made an executive decision and decided to save the room at the end of the hall for last. It was clear that it would take more manpower to get the thing open anyways so we about faced and headed back down the stairs where Nichols was waiting for us.

"Find anything up there?" he asked.

"No bodies, but we're not done. We're going to need to head back once you show me these corpses. Where's the rest of your team?"

"Waiting for us in the basement with the prisoner."

"Prisoner!?"

Nichols glanced over his shoulder, directing my attention to the hidden door they had found. "Yeah. There's some kind of holding cell down there. The only one alive is the guy that was locked up, but that's not all you need to see."

We followed Nichols and Diaz down to the basement of the compound where the other two members of their team were already waiting for us. To say the stench in that small compact room was unpleasant would be have been an understatement. The smell of the decomposing bodies lining the cellar floor was overpowering. I could feel my stomach begin to toss and turn, but fought hard to suppress the queasy sensation. As the team leader, I knew how important it was to keep it together in front of the boys. If they see you're off your game, then they won't be able to trust you to make calls when their lives are on the line.

There were eight of us down there – team I was leading and the one I had put Nichols in charge of all sharing a small space littered with corpses. Needless to say, it was beginning to feel cramped. I instructed four soldiers back to the gate in order to free up elbow-room and provide Horrowitz with a little more support. It was now just Nichols, Diaz, Barker (a weapons sergeant who had been part of my original team) and myself.

On the far end of the cellar was a heavy metal door that joined a much smaller connecting room. At the base of the door was a small window that allowed guards to pass food, water, and waste in and out of the jail cell. Just like the gate, the door was fastened with a chain and a single padlock. I stepped over the bodies, slid open the small window, and took a look inside the cell. Sitting on the floor was an Afghan male who appeared to be in his mid to late thirties. He was dressed in the traditional garb of the people who resided in the area and sported the typical chinstrap beard that was worn by many of his fellow countrymen. His body was rail-thin, as if his muscles had wasted away, yet he seemed unfazed by this. He was alert and upright, if anything almost a little bored by our presence. All in all, there was nothing particularly off-putting about the way he looked, but for some reason, watching him brought out the same terrible feeling of dread I had been experiencing upstairs.

Nichols could tell I was curious about the prisoner. "I've been questioning him about what went down here, but he's not talking. You can try yourself if you want."

I turned my head back towards Nichols, "What do you think went down here?"

"Don't know, but whatever happened was weird as shit."

"What are you talking about?" I asked.

"Open your eyes, Willi! Look at these bodies." Nichols got down to one knee and extended a finger to the neck of one of the corpses. "This looks like an exit wound from a .22. Every single one of these corpses has the exact same hole in the front of the neck. Check yourself if you don't believe me. Naturally, at first I assumed this was some kind of execution, but look!" He yanked so hard on the rotting stiff's head to lift it that I was surprised he didn't pull it off. "No entry point at the back of the neck. It's like the fucking bullet was fired from inside the guy's throat."

"My theory is the bullet entered from the front of the neck and Nichols is getting his panties riled up about nothing." Diaz said from the corner of the room.

"Yeah, its not surprising an idiot like you would come up with a theory like that. See how the skin and the muscle seem to stray outward? It's clear something came out of this hole not in it. Even if it had entered here, don't you think at least one of these guys would have an exit wound, Willi?"

"It's curious, but we don't really have time to speculate right now. We weren't sent here to play CSI and Horrowitz needs the rest of us outside. Snap some photos, grab the prisoner and lets get out of here."

"Grab the prisoner?" Nichols looked stunned. "What, are we taking P.O.W's now? How can we be sure he's not one of the guys we were sent here to hit?"

"And how can we be sure he's not a friendly?" I said. "He was locked up when you got here so we know someone put him in the cell. He certainly didn't lock himself away."

Nichols shook his head, "No, no, no, the guy's giving me a bad vibe, Willi–"

"I don't really give a damn what kind of vibe he's giving you. We don't just kill people because they give us the *heebie jeebies*. He looks like he's in need of medical attention. We're not leaving him here." To be honest, the prisoner was making me more than a little uncomfortable. There was something wholly unpleasant in the air and I couldn't help but feel like it was radiating from that cell. I had made up my mind though.

"This is bullshit!" Nichols shoved a gloved finger into my chest. "We had our orders. We're here to terminate any POTENTIAL terrorist threat in this facility! That guy feels like bad news and you know it. Let's take him out and be done with it. Last I checked, we weren't told anything about bringing back P.O.W's. I mean think about it. How thick could your skull really be? These corpses on the floor have been dead for weeks – months maybe, they should be nothing but bones by now. Why are they rotting so slowly? Plus, even if they did lock him up, how the hell is he not a corpse yet too? Who's feeding him' or cleaning up his shit for that matter?"

"Stand down!" I fired back. "Last I checked I was Papa Sierra of this outfit. You got a problem with that, fine. We can discuss it later, but we are getting that prisoner out of this basement right now. That's an order. Now get that lock cut!"

Diaz cut the lock using the same pair of bolt cutters that we used to get past the gate. He and Barker entered the cell, grabbed the prisoner firmly by each arm, and hoisted him to his feet. Standing between the two soldiers, he looked mind numbingly skinny. I remember thinking how he wasn't just swimming in his baggy robes – he was drowning in them. I wondered if he'd even be able to walk. Nichols didn't protest as Diaz and Barker dragged him out of the cell and into the room, but he didn't have to. I could see the disapproving look in his eyes.

The sudden sound of gunshots erupting upstairs broke the tension between us. There was no need to bark orders; everyone in that basement knew Horrowitz and the rest of our unit needed as much support as they could get. I took point and lead us up the stairs followed closely behind by Nichols while Diaz and Barker, still holding on to either arm of the prisoner, brought up the rear. By the time I reached the top, shots were still tearing through the mountain air. I was already starting out the door when I heard a *CRASH* behind me. I whirled around just in time to see Barker and Diaz fall to the floor as the prisoner sprinted up to the facility's second level. Somehow the sickly looking man had been able to toss two Green Berets in their physical prime aside like they were children and was making an escape. Without missing a beat, Nichols took off up the steps after him.

"Diaz!" I shouted. "Go with him and meet us outside." He gave chase while Barker and I hauled ass to the front gate where we found Horrowitz and the rest of the team hunkered down behind the walls.

The villagers had launched a full on assault on my unit. Flashes of light flickered in the darkness as a hail of gun-storm rained down on us. Our attackers almost seemed to meld into the shadows, disappearing behind cover every time we fired back. It didn't take long to realize they had been trained – even the children.

Horrowitz looked relieved to see me. I don't think he wanted to be the one who made the call to air support. "They didn't start shootn' till they noticed the group comn' outta the buildn'!"

"Nichols and Diaz should be right behind us," I said. "I'm calling the choppers right now!"

My radio's connection was shoddy at best, but I was able to get a hold of the pilots. The birds were about ten minutes away. I instructed everyone to stay sharp, lay low, and fend off our attackers until they showed up. I tried Nichols and Diaz over the com since they hadn't made it out of the facility yet, but neither answered.

"We need to get 'em outta that buildn'!" Shouted Horrowtiz over the shots. "There's a good chance the gunners on those choppers might start shootn' up the compound. It *is* our target, after all."

He was right. When I radioed for help, the mountains had been playing hell with our signal. I tried to warn air support not to hit the building, but I had no way of knowing if they got the entire message.

Nichols and Diaz still hadn't made it out, and I couldn't risk them getting caught in there when the helicopters showed up so I left Horrowitz at the gate and instructed Barker to follow me back inside to look for them.

The unbearable humidity in the air had nothing on the crushing sense of desperation whirling through my mind as we made our way through the upstairs rooms for the second time that evening. The choppers were coming. That much I knew, but what I didn't know was whether or not we'd still be inside when they were leveling the building.

I had expected to hear Nichols or Diaz's boots stomping around once we reached the second level, but the place was eerily silent. Just like before, Barker and I moved from empty room to empty room making our way towards the oversized door at the end of the hall with the bizarre markings engraved into it. Time was short. We hustled over to it but paused when we realized that it had been opened – a tiny trickle of light leaked out from the crack in the door. I turned towards Barker, his face, a mask of uncertainty.

"Barker," I said. "Am I crazy or were we not able to get this door open earlier?"

"You're not crazy, sir. We tried, but couldn't get it open."

The sound of helicopter blades spinning through the air started to bleed into my ears.

Barker grabbed me around my arm. "The choppers are here! We need to hurry up and get the hell out of here!"

But I shook him off and told him we weren't leaving without the rest of the team.

There was no more time to take precautions. I burst into the room with little regard for my personal safety. And as soon as I did, I felt my reservations about the assignment magnify ten fold.

The room that had been hidden behind the door was quite a bit different from the rest of the facility. More bizarre symbols had been carved into the wooden floors – hieroglyphics and weird patterns, peculiar cryptic shapes that I had never seen before, all forming a semi circle that spanned nearly half the room, facing the western wall. Candles were everywhere – their flames had long been snuffed out before our arrival, leaving only melted disfigured forms behind, like the lowly unfortunate survivors of a horrific nuclear attack. Nichols and Diaz were standing in the center of the room, the prisoner's dead body sprawled across the floor at their feet. The choppers blades grew louder.

"Let's go!" I shouted. "Everybody out now!"

Nichols and Diaz remained in place, statuesque, cold, looking apathetic and indifferent. Their faces were expressionless. I rushed into the room and shoved them towards the door.

"What the hell is wrong with you!? Didn't you hear me!? I said get out now!"

That was enough to get them moving. They followed Barker into the hall and down the stairs. I started out after them, but something caught my eye. Books bound in leather laid open on a rusty old metal table. They looked to be religious texts, but not Islamic. In their pages were bizarre drawings of otherworldly creatures and more of the same strange hieroglyphics that had been carved into the floor. Next to one of the leather bound books was a note pad. On the paper, there was a message written in Arabic.

It came from the heavens, but brings hell upon this world. It breeds. It is not human, but it hides inside us.

Those last nine words made me feel sick. I looked over at the prisoner's body, still face down on the floor and suddenly I was reminded that I was now alone.

It is not human...

I took a step towards the corpse, half expecting it to spring back to life.

But it...

The choppers blades were even louder now, but my radio was getting nothing but static. I couldn't even reach the rest of my team. Gunshots were still crackling outside and I prayed none of my guys had been hit.

hides inside us...

When I got close enough I slid the toe of my boot under the dead prisoner's torso and flipped it over. In the front of his neck was a hole identical to the ones we had found on the corpses in the basement.

I'm not entirely sure how long I stared at the prisoner, trying to process what on Earth was going on. Questions were swirling through my head. What the hell had Nichols and Diaz been doing in there? I fought the itch to look around the room for answers, deciding I'd be pushing my luck if I stayed in that place much longer. The next thing I knew I was sprinting down the stairs of the facility and out the front door just as the choppers started filling it full of shells. A few seconds earlier and they would have taken me down along with the facility.

The villagers were still firing on my team when I got back to the wall. Thankfully, we hadn't taken any casualties yet. Soon after, the black hawks buzzed over our heads and began raining down bullets on the Afghan village. Their choppers' heavy-duty artillery easily leveled the little huts and swatted our attackers away like gnats. Hot shells sliced through the bodies of men and boy's alike, as the area around the compound became a scene of absolute carnage. In all my years working Special Ops it was definitely the most violent altercation I have ever been involved in.

Once the choppers had landed and it was safe to board we left the cover of the compound walls and made our way back to the birds. I'm rarely taken aback by the aftermath of a skirmish, but the village and the area around it had been completely obliterated. Horrowitz, Barker, and four other members of my unit entered one of the choppers while Nichols, Diaz, myself and the rest of my team crossed the battlefield to get in the other.

We were about 20 meters from the helicopters when I felt something snag my ankle. I spun around to see an elderly bearded man on ground the trying to tell me something. His body had been riddled with bullets and he was bleeding profusely from multiple wounds. I could tell it was only a matter of time before his organs would begin shutting down on him. He looked up to me and opened his mouth to speak. I don't know exactly why I bent down to hear him better. Perhaps it was the expression in his eyes. I've seen the look on a man's face when he's about to die. It's usually one of panic; sometimes regret, or sadness, occasionally peace, but this man's eyes showed only that of concern.

His words were faint. The old man did his very best to get them out, but he was saying things in Farsi that I couldn't understand. Some of the words I recognized, but before I could ask him to clarify, the sound of Nichol's .45 boomed through the air, and silenced him. I looked up, furious that he had just put a bullet in the dying man's head.

"I put him out of his misery," Nichols said. "He was going to die anyways." We boarded the chopper and took off from that god-awful place on our way back to HQ.

During the flight, I pulled out a piece of notebook paper from my bag and wrote down phonetically what I heard the villager say before Nichols shot him.

"Do you know what this means Nichols?" I asked. "That man said it to me before you shot him." I repeated what I wrote down.

It was then that I noticed the look in Diaz's eyes. He was still relatively new to my unit, but I had read his file and as far as I know he couldn't speak a lick of Farsi. His face told me a different story. Diaz looked like a cheating lover getting outed by his spouse. Nichols seemed bothered too. He took the paper from me and asked me to repeat what I heard. When I complied, he snickered, tore it in two, and tossed it aside.

"Pfft, it's nothing, sir. Just some garbage about Westerners being filthy pigs."

"What were you and Diaz doing in the room upstairs, Nichols? And why was it locked?"

Nichols scratched at the stubble on his chin. "The prisoner attacked us in there, sir. I don't know what he was thinking. He was aggressive and Diaz and I were forced to fire on him."

"He was unarmed," I said. Nichols shrugged. "I checked out the body. The hole in the prisoner's neck was identical to the corpses in the basement. Can you explain that?"

"Yeah," Nichol's said. "I guess I was wrong about my initial assessment of the situation. I popped him in the neck. The bullet didn't pass all the way through, sir."

Sir.

He said it again. Nichols never called me that on missions, only in front of superiors. His story sounded like a bunch of horseshit, but I assumed he was just trying to cover for Diaz and himself. As far as I was concerned he had just shot and killed an unarmed man because he didn't like the vibe he was getting from him. We remained quiet the rest of the way back, only breaking the silence with occasional one word answers when the pilots would ask us a question.

I could still remember the phonetic spelling of what that villager had said. After we landed, I slipped away for a moment and wrote it down again. As curious as I was about following up on it, the villager's last words became a trivial concern to me due to the fact that I was more worried about Diaz and Nichols actions with the prisoner.

I excluded the bit about them shooting him and just reported that everyone in the facility was dead upon our arrival. To be honest, it was more to save my hide than theirs. The last thing I needed was for my unit to get sidelined while the Washington bureaucrats launched some needlessly long investigation.

Diaz went home to Los Angeles for some "R&R" just a couple weeks later. That was the last time I ever saw him. He went AWOL after that and never returned to duty. Nichols would retire from military life just months after that and head back to his hometown just outside Charleston, NC. The strange thing was, he only stayed briefly before collecting some things and disappearing off the face of the Earth. Even his family didn't know where he had gone. Nichols was young and for as long as I had known the guy he was a career man looking to climb the ranks so his departure from active duty just seemed sudden.

About seven years after Nichols disappearance, Diaz's dead body was found in a gas station restroom off the side of I-40 in Oklahoma. It had the same hole in the front of the neck as the prisoner and the insurgents in the basement. I along with every member of my unit that the government could locate was called in for questioning about that night. They all stuck to the original story I put in my report – everyone was dead when we arrived.

I was given an early severance package and let go from the military. It was a unique situation. One day I was commanding my own special ops unit and the next I was a civilian. I did get to keep all my veteran benefits thankfully.

I still see some of the boys every now and then. Horrowitz and I grab a beer (or nine) together whenever he's in town. It was a discussion I had with him on one of these nights that has caused me to sometimes question my sanity whenever I think about what really happened between Diaz, Nichols, and the prisoner in that room.

We were out drinking at a local watering hole, watching the football game that was playing on the bar's TV. It was my turn to pay for the round. When I pulled out my wallet and opened it up, I caught a glimpse of a folded up piece of paper sticking out of one of the side pockets. It was the very same paper I had written down the dying old villager's words on when the helicopter picked us up. Horrowitz spoke Farsi better than anyone I knew so I decided to read it out to him.

"What?" He laughed after I read it. "Are you sure you heard that right?"

"Yeah," I said. "Nichols told me that it was something about Westerners being filthy pigs."

Horrowitz shook his head, "Well then Nichols, wherever he is, needs to pick up Rosetta Stone 'cause that sure as hell ain't what you just said."

"I didn't think so," I said. "The very first thing you learn when you're over there is all the good insults and curse words and *this* was one I hadn't heard before."

"That's 'cause it ain't no insult. It sounds more like a warning, but it doesn't make a whole lotta' sense. That's why I asked if you heard it right."

"I know what I heard." I insisted. "What's it mean?"

"Well," Horrowitz leaned back in his chair and took a sip of beer. "If you're sure that's what you heard, then what that villager said is this: It came from the stars. It cannot be killed, but it can be contained. Do not release the parasite or it will breed and spread."

Want More?

Make sure to check out Vincent V. Cava's:

Decomposing Head:

Frighteningly Funny Tales That Will Rot Your Brain

Written by the authors of several Top 100 Kindle eBooks (in their darkly comedic and satirical genres):

Here you have found a book so foul, so repulsive, so horrifying... that you will undoubtedly find yourself running to the nearest bathroom in an effort to both relieve your bowels and scrub your hands clean of its putrid filth. Though these attempts will be in vain -- just as the authors of this demented book of short stories have planned. I speak of none other than the intolerable Mr. Vincent V. Cava and his dimwitted pen pal, S.R. Tooms (the pair oftentimes billed simply as Hideous and Handsome). They have finally released this humorous collection of terrifying tales, despite the bitter public outcry which demanded these pages never see the light of day... and perhaps for good reason.

Inside this tome you will read such stories as the much talked about "Gas Station Bathroom," which has been known to cause many travelers to rethink their next rest stop pullover.

The psychological masterpiece in "The Horror of Knowing" will never allow you to gaze upon your friends in the same light again.

"A Favor for a Favor" depicts an unparalleled moralistic look at the true nature of mankind -- complete with an exquisitely satisfying finish that will have you shaking your head with sinister disbelief.

These are but a few of the many finely crafted tales lurking within this haunted collection. To those of you with a few screws loose in the noggin or those with a twisted smile (and crooked tooth or two), I bid you enter this haven of horror...

Just A Little Terrible

Just a little...
Haunting – These tomes of terror will stay with you long after you put your book down and go to bed for the evening. They've been known to burrow themselves into a reader's imagination and are capable of warping dreams into twisted, unspeakable   nightmares.

Just a little...

Unique — These aren't your standard horror stories. Don't think this collection will include tales of haunted mansions, or blood sucking vampires. Expect one-of-a-kind takes on every gothic ghoul and hideous monster you read about in this book.

Just a little...

Frightening – Prepare yourself for some of the most chilling flash fiction ever penned. The mad genius, Vincent V. Cava, has done it again with the latest entry in his creepy catalogue. Do yourself a favor and leave the lights on when you read it.

Just A Little... **Terrible**

Dead Connection

Reader beware!

The stories that lurk within the pages of this book will have you **cowering under the covers in fear**, praying that the shadows shifting underneath your closet door are nothing more than an optical illusion.

Delve into the depraved minds of horror's newest authors in this chilling collection of tales.

Made in the USA
Lexington, KY
19 November 2016